Thierry isn't a chicken shifter — he's a French hen shifter. He won't let anyone call him a chicken, not even if the person doing it is a gorgeous man who saved him from a vicious attack. Okay, maybe not so vicious, since the fox who tried to eat Thierry was the man's five-year-old niece, but still. Bishop is as infuriating as he is kiss-worthy, and Thierry isn't planning on talking to him ever again.

And he doesn't, until he tells his mother Bishop is his boyfriend and that he'll bring him home for Christmas.

Bishop knows where he went wrong with Thierry, so when they meet again because Thierry's car breaks down, he apologizes. He might enjoy getting a rise out of the gorgeous man, but he doesn't want Thierry to hate him.

Apparently, Thierry doesn't, since he told his mother they were dating.

They aren't, although Bishop can easily imagine them together, even though he shouldn't. He promised his sister he would always take care of her when their parents died, and he hasn't changed his mind.

Is there space for Bishop's sister, his niece, and Thierry in his life — and in his heart? Or will Bishop have to choose and possibly ruin Christmas for everyone, including himself?

Have a Foxy Christmas
Copyright © 2020 Catherine Lievens
ISBN: 978-1-4874-3167-9
Cover art by Martine Jardin

Published by eXtasy Books Inc or
Devine Destinies, an imprint of eXtasy Books Inc

Look for us online at:
www.eXtasybooks.com or www.devinedestinies.com

Have a Foxy Christmas

By

Catherine Lievens

CHAPTER ONE

Bishop looked at the little girl who was playing in front of him. When he'd agreed to babysit for his sister, he hadn't thought it would be this complicated. He should have known better, since Carly was Ivy's daughter. Of course it was complicated.

She looked just like Ivy, too, with her long brown hair caught in a messy braid and her big brown eyes that looked at Bishop as if he were a monster who didn't understand why only apple juice was okay.

"Are you sure you don't want orange juice? There's no apple juice left," he tried.

Carly looked like she was about to break down crying, and Bishop blamed himself. Blaming himself for not knowing the apple juice was finished wouldn't help, though, and he took a deep breath.

"I want apple juice," Carly said.

She was only five, but she knew what she wanted and when she wanted it. She's gotten that from Ivy, too.

Bishop had to get out of the situation. "Why don't we do this," he started, frantically trying to find a solution before the crying began. "Drink some of the orange juice. I know it's not your favorite, but it's all there is. Then, we'll go play outside."

That got Carly's attention. "And I can be my fox?" she asked.

She was too adorable for her own good, and Bishop had to work hard not to smile. "You can shift in your fox form, but only if you drink the orange juice or milk, or even water. And

1

you can't cry because we don't have apple juice. I'll put it on the grocery list so your mom knows about it, but there's nothing else I can do right now."

It only took Carly a few seconds to decide she was fine with the orange juice and reach for it. Bishop relinquished it, sighing in relief.

He'd hoped things would go this way. Carly was always eager to shift, but that was hard, with all the humans around. She'd been taught since she was a newborn that she couldn't shift whenever she wanted, which was one of the reasons Ivy had bought this house. It had a yard, but it was well protected, so no one would see into it. Carly could shift into her fox form to her little heart's content, run around, and have fun. That was a good thing, because it was the only way for her to learn to control the shift and move as a fox, but it still made Bishop nervous. The yard might be protected from curious gazes, but they were still in the middle of town, and someone could possibly see them. If that happened, it would be a disaster.

Human beings didn't know about shifters, and things had to stay that way. Bishop had seen enough movies and read enough books to know what would happen if they found out shifters existed. Then, shifters would become lab experiments, and just the thought of his niece in a cage made Bishop want to hit something. He would do everything he could to make sure that didn't happen, even if it meant giving Carly less freedom.

He didn't have to, though. Ivy had recently bought this house, and Carly had enough space and privacy to shift whenever she wanted.

Carly drank down her juice as fast as she could, then handed the empty box back to Bishop. Bishop shook his head, amused, and took it. "Wash your hands. Then we can head outside—as long as your room is neat."

Carly bit her lower lip, probably thinking about whether or

not her room would qualify as neat. She seemed to decide it would and hopped off the chair to go wash her hands, leaving Bishop behind without a second glance.

While she was in the bathroom, Bishop quickly cleaned the kitchen. They were alone in the house today, but it still looked like a bomb had exploded all over the place. The plates from lunch were still in the sink, but he would rinse them and put them in the dishwasher later. For now, he had a promise to keep.

As soon as Carly was back from the bathroom, they headed outside. It was cold, but Carly didn't seem to care much as she quickly stripped. She dumped her clothes on the ground, and Bishop cleared his throat, pointedly looking at them.

"You know better," he said when she just stared.

Carly huffed. She grabbed her t-shirt and put it on the bench that was there for just that reason. Then she picked up the rest of her clothes. "I'm going to put them on again. Why do I have to fold them?" she asked.

"You shouldn't treat your belongings that way." Although since her idea of folding her clothes was to roll them into a tight ball, maybe being thrown on the ground wasn't that bad. "Now go on. Shift. I know you want to."

Carly grinned at him, then shifted. Her fox form was tiny, at least to Bishop's eyes, and extremely adorable. She launched herself into the yard, yapping at a few pigeons, running around in a circle as she tried to catch her tail. She acted more like a dog than a fox, and Bishop hoped she would use most of her energy playing. That way, she would go down easy tonight.

He leaned back against the wall of the house, keeping an eye on Carly. She was cute as she played, and he was grateful he could do this for her and Ivy. He'd missed them when they hadn't lived here, but now he had them back, and he was part of their family again.

He hadn't truly lost them, though. Ivy had met a man, and she'd tried to make things work. She'd even moved to be with him, and Bishop hadn't tried to stop her. He had to protect her, but he couldn't force her to do anything, and he'd known that nothing he could say would dissuade her. He hadn't liked that guy, and he'd kept an eye on him, so he hadn't been that surprised to find out he was cheating on Ivy.

But that was in the past now. Bishop had his family back, even though it was crippled. It wasn't his entire family, but it was all the family he had since his and Ivy's parents had died, and he would make sure nothing happened to Ivy and Carly. He couldn't allow it. They had to be his entire focus. Ivy was still hurting over losing their parents, and she was trying to find her way in life, and Bishop had to be her rock. He had been for a long time, and that wasn't going to change anytime soon.

Having Ivy close would help with that, he thought as he looked up.

Carly was gone. His eyes widened as he looked around the yard, knowing she couldn't be far. "Carly?" he called out, panic rising in his chest. It threatened to take over, to make it hard to think and even harder to breathe.

He pushed it down. She couldn't have left the yard. He would have noticed if she had, right?

But he'd been distracted.

"Carly? Where are you? If you're hiding, it's not funny."

She didn't answer.

He moved to search the yard. He wasn't about to call his sister to tell her that her daughter had disappeared. She had to be here somewhere. She knew she couldn't leave the yard, and she was going to get a timeout if she had, but she wasn't stupid. She was aware of what would happen if humans found out she was a shifter, and she was usually careful.

Usually, but not now, because she was gone.

4

Thierry was chilling in his backyard when he was attacked.

He wasn't sure what happened. One second, he was strutting around in his hen form, enjoying the cold weather, and the next, a fox jumped on him. Thierry squawked and flapped his wings, hoping it would stop the fox from trying to munch on him. It did, but only for a moment. Then, the fox tried to catch him again.

That was when he realized the fox was a baby.

He squawked, then flew up to the patio table. He settled on the edge, looking down at the fox with narrow eyes.

It wasn't a baby fox like he'd first thought, but it was a young fox, and Thierry had no idea how it had ended up in his yard. He wanted to ask, but of course, the fox couldn't answer, and he couldn't form words in his hen form anyway.

Besides, the fox was staring up at him as if it wanted to eat him, and it probably did. It had sat and didn't seem to be about to try to get to Thierry, but it also didn't seem like it was going to leave anytime soon.

Thierry frowned. There weren't usually foxes in the area, which made him wonder where this one had come from. He'd bought his house because even though there were houses on both sides, the yard was isolated by tall hedges, and the porch was big enough that he could shift there without anyone seeing him from the upstairs windows of the other houses. It was the only reason he'd felt free to shift.

He looked more closely. The cub wagged its tail, so it either wanted to eat him or play with him—possibly both.

Thierry was okay with neither. He didn't want to be eaten, and he didn't want to play. He didn't appreciate being attacked in his yard. He had no idea where the fox had come from, but he wanted it to leave, and he wanted it to leave now.

"Carly?" a man called out.

Thierry squawked again when he noticed the man coming through the hedge. What the fuck was happening? Where was he coming from? He was obviously a neighbor, but he shouldn't have been able to move through the hedge the way he was. Thierry was going to have to call someone tomorrow and put up a wall or something like that between the properties. He did *not* want people to walk in on him when he was in his hen form. It could lead to a disaster, and he didn't want to become a circus phenomenon or a lab experiment.

The man's gaze stopped on the fox, and he sucked in a breath. "Carly. Here you are. You scared me to death." He rushed toward the fox, and Thierry blinked.

Well, at least the man who'd invaded his privacy was a good-looking one. He was tall, with wide shoulders, and Thierry could see tattoos peeking from the collar of his sweater. His short hair was dark, as were his eyes, and heavy stubble covered his cheeks. His ears were pierced, and Thierry found himself wanting to lick a path up the man's neck and see how the rings would feel under his tongue.

No. Bad French hen. Thierry had to focus on what was happening, not on what he wanted to do to this man.

The man barely even looked at him. Instead, he leaned down and grabbed the fox, raising it and holding it up to his face. "You know you shouldn't escape the yard. Your mom was clear about that, and so was I. You can play in your fox form in the yard, but that's it. No one can see you. It's dangerous."

Thierry blinked again. Had the man just said fox form?

Thierry looked at the cub, puppy, or whatever they called it. There was no way for him to know whether or not the cub was a shifter, but given what the man had said, he suspected that was the case. That probably meant the man was a shifter, too, and Thierry would have been smiling if he'd been in his human form. He had shifter neighbors. What were the odds?

But whatever they were, he didn't want these people in his yard. He didn't want to be attacked by a fox, shifter or not.

The cub suddenly shifted in the man's hands. She was older than Thierry had expected, although since he didn't have experience with children, that wasn't surprising. "I'm sorry, Uncle Bishop," the girl said with a sob. "I didn't want to be naughty. I just wanted to see what was on this side of the hedge."

The man — Uncle Bishop — relaxed. "There's no need to cry. I know you didn't mean anything by it, but it's dangerous. It's especially dangerous because you attacked the neighbors' chicken. What would happen if you'd hurt it? And if someone had been in the house and noticed you? They could have killed you, Carly. You *have* to be careful."

Thierry shared that opinion, but he was offended at being called a chicken. The man wasn't even looking at him, but he shifted, finding himself sitting naked on the edge of the table. The surface was freezing, but he did his best to ignore it. The girl's — Carly — eyes went wide as she took in Thierry.

"I am *not* a chicken," Thierry snapped. "And stop scaring that little girl. Give her some clothes, too. She must be freezing." Thierry certainly was.

The man twirled around, clutching the girl to his chest. "Holy shit."

Thierry crossed his arms over his chest. "I'm not a chicken," he repeated. "I'm a French hen. A Faverolle."

Uncle Bishop didn't seem to have an answer to that. He stared at Thierry, and Thierry straightened his back. He knew he didn't look bad, even when he was naked. He wasn't as tall and muscled as Bishop was under his clothes, but he could hold his own, even in a fight.

He hoped it wouldn't come to that, though. He also hoped the man *was* a shifter. There was no way for him to know, but since he was holding a fox shifter and she'd called him uncle, there were good chances he was a fox shifter, too.

And Thierry was a French hen.

Merde. What had he gotten himself into?

Chapter Two

The chicken was a shifter, and apparently, he didn't like being called a chicken. Bishop had no idea what a French hen was, but to him, the guy had looked like a chicken. Bishop was ready to admit it was a pretty one, though. His feathers were a light beige, most of them the same color with only a few lighter or darker. And of course, the flappy thing on his head was bright red.

Now, he looked like a naked guy, and Bishop didn't know where to look. He was pretty sure the guy would kill him if he noticed Bishop ogling his body, no matter how gorgeous he was.

"I'm not scaring her," he explained. "I'm just trying to warn her. She was lucky this time, because you're a shifter. She might not be as lucky the next time."

The man on the table grimaced. "All right. I can see that."

Bishop had to force himself to look at Carly rather than at the guy because the man was ridiculously attractive. He was shorter than Bishop—that much was obvious, even though he was sitting down, and where Bishop was dark with brown hair, tan skin, and full of tattoos, this guy was light. He was blond, and while his eyes were brown, they were light enough to look almost amber in the daylight. He was not as muscular as Bishop, which was perfect, because Bishop had never been attracted to muscular guys who looked like him.

But he wasn't focusing on the things he should focus on.

He swallowed again, wondering what was next. He should take Carly home, but he couldn't seem to be able to move.

Luckily for him, Carly shifted to her fox form again, grabbing his attention, and Bishop held her closer. He tried to soothe her. Even though he'd been terrified, he shouldn't have scolded her as brusquely as he had. It was his fault that she'd run away, not hers. She was only five, and she wanted to explore. He should have kept a better eye on her.

"I'm sorry we barged onto your property," he finally said. "It won't happen again."

The guy looked at Carly, then back at Bishop. "Good. She scared me."

A flash of guilt tore through Bishop. "I'm really sorry." He turned his attention back to Carly. "You can't hunt chickens, Carly, or any other animal. You were lucky because Mr. here was a shifter. What's going to happen if you hurt chickens that belong to a human? What if the owners see you? I know you didn't mean to hurt anyone, but you have to be careful, sweetheart."

"I am *not* a chicken. I'm a French hen. I told you that," the guy snapped.

It was kind of amusing, and Bishop couldn't deny that he was saying the guy was a chicken to get a rise out of him. He turned toward the guy again. "I'm sorry. I have no idea what a French hen is." But he was going to Google it as soon as he was out of sight. "I'm Bishop. I'd shake your hand, but as you can see, both are full."

The man looked at him, then nodded curtly. "I'm Thierry."

The name sounded French, and since the guy was a French hen like he'd already said twice, he was probably not from the US. Not that Bishop cared about that. Hell, he couldn't seem to care about anything that wasn't the guy's body right now.

He cleared his throat. "I don't understand the difference. You looked like a chicken when I came through here. And aren't hens a type of chicken?"

Thierry's eyes narrowed, and he hopped off the table.

Bishop jerked his gaze up so he wouldn't be staring at Thierry's cock, although before he did so, he got a glimpse, and then, he couldn't wait to get his hands on it.

What the fuck is wrong with me?

Not only did he have to work hard not to stare at Thierry — and not to let the man see how much he found him attractive and appealing — but he was also delighted by Thierry's scowl and enjoyed making him angry. He never behaved this way, and he didn't understand what was going on. It couldn't just be that Thierry was sexy as fuck, right? His cheeks had pinked when he'd gotten angry, and his eyes were blazing, and it made Bishop want to shift and beg for belly rubs.

"You know where the gate is," Thierry snapped.

"I didn't come in through the gate."

"Well, you can go back from where you came from. I don't want you on my property. You're offending me, and I won't just stand here and allow you to do that."

"I didn't mean to offend you," Bishop said even though it was partly a lie. "I was just saying things the way I see them."

"And I'm telling you things the way *I* see them, which is that you're rude and that I don't want to see you on my property again." His gaze shifted to Carly, who was cowering against Bishop's chest. "She, on the other hand, is welcome to come around any time she wants."

Bishop couldn't help the huff of laughter that escaped him. "Really? She attacked you, yet she's welcome, while I called you a chicken and you kick me out?"

"I'm kicking you out because you didn't listen to me, and you continued calling me a chicken even though I told you that's not what I am. Goodbye."

There was nothing else for Bishop to do except leave. He couldn't stop smiling as he did so, though. He was amused by Thierry's offended expression. And yes, he'd done it on purpose. He knew what he was doing when he'd called Thierry a chicken. It was obvious that getting his breed right was important for Thierry, but instead of doing that, Bishop had been poking and prodding until he got a rise out of him.

It didn't matter anyway. It was probably the last time he and Thierry would see each other. Bishop was going to do his best so that Carly couldn't sneak into the neighbor's yard again, and he would be more careful. Ivy and Carly were the only family he had left. He wasn't going to mess things up. He couldn't allow himself to mess things up, not again.

He had to focus on them.

By the time he got home, Ivy was back. She was in the kitchen, putting things into the fridge from a grocery bag, and she turned around when she heard them. She arched a brow when she saw that Carly was in her fox form. "You weren't outside in the yard when I came back," she said.

"That's because little Miss Carly here escaped into the neighbor's yard. Did you know he was a shifter?" he asked as he put Carly down. She scampered away, no doubt headed to her room.

"He is? I didn't know. I haven't had the time to meet the neighbors yet. What did he say?"

"Well, our first introduction wasn't great, since he's a chicken—no, a French hen shifter. She saw him and jumped on him. She wanted to play, but I think she freaked him out."

Ivy chuckled. "Of course she did. He probably thought she was a fox and that she was going to eat him."

That made Bishop feel guilty. He'd been making fun of Thierry, but now that he thought about it, he realized Thierry probably had actually been scared. Foxes were chickens' natural predators, and Thierry was in the middle of the city, in his own yard. He probably hadn't expected a fox to jump on him and try to eat him, even though that wasn't what Carly had been attempting to do.

"How is he?" Ivy asked. Her eyes glinted, and Bishop knew what she was thinking about.

He shook his head. "I don't know. Prissy and stuck up, I guess." And he was. No matter how fun it had been to get a rise out of him, Bishop didn't think they would ever get along if they saw each other again. The fact that he could too easily imagine Thierry in his bed didn't change that fact.

They were too different. It wasn't just because Bishop had to focus on his family and forget about men. It was also that they were fox and chicken, that Thierry didn't seem to know how to have fun, and that he was easily offended. It was because Bishop liked to tease people, and he wasn't going to change himself for anyone, least of all a man he couldn't have.

"I don't like him," he said.

Ivy didn't look convinced. "If you say so. He didn't yell at Carly, did he?"

"No. Actually, he defended her when I scolded her for running away and attacking a chicken. He doesn't like to be called that, by the way."

"Of course he doesn't. You don't like being called a dog."

"That's because I'm *not* a dog. I'm a fox. They're different species. French hens are chickens, no matter what he says."

Ivy leaned back against the counter and crossed her arms over her chest. "You seem particularly prickly when it comes to this guy. How come?"

Bishop shook his head. "I told you. I don't like him." And he hoped he would never see the guy again. He didn't want to.

Or at least, that was what he tried to convince himself.

Thierry stumbled inside the house, abandoning his clothes on the porch. How dare that man? He'd called Thierry a chicken several times, even after Thierry had explained that he was *not* one. He was one of the most infuriating men Thierry had the displeasure of knowing, and Thierry wanted to punch him in that smug face of his.

Thierry grabbed one of the blankets on the couch and wrapped it around his shoulders. It was too cold to go around naked, especially outside. He felt chilled down to his bones, and he knew he shouldn't have shifted. He normally wouldn't have, but the situation had been anything but normal.

He flopped onto the couch, leaning his head against it. That man had been infuriating, and Thierry wanted to go back out there and force him to admit that he wasn't a chicken.

Chickens were food. Thierry refused to eat them, but still. No one would think about eating him or any other French hen shifters. They weren't food. They were beautiful hens, and some of Thierry's ancestors had won beauty contests. Of course, Thierry's new neighbor wouldn't know about that. He wouldn't know about anything that had to do with Faverolles.

He hadn't even introduced himself. He'd been rude, and Thierry wasn't surprised. Bishop *looked* like he would be rude.

He also looked like he would be great in bed, though.

Thierry sucked in a breath. He couldn't think about that. As far as he was concerned, he and Bishop were mortal enemies. As long as Bishop wouldn't admit that Thierry wasn't a chicken, things would stay that way. Besides, he wasn't Thierry's usual type. He was too big. He had massive shoulders that looked like Thierry would be able to hang onto them as they had sex. He had a lot of tattoos that Thierry wanted to trace with his tongue. He had eyes that Thierry wanted to lose himself in.

None of that would happen.

Thierry was going to stick with safe, preppy, gentlemen. He didn't have a boyfriend right now, and he wasn't planning on finding one, but if he ever wanted a one-night stand, he knew where to find the kind of guys he was looking for.

And it wasn't next door.

He sighed. For whatever reason, he couldn't stop thinking about what little he'd seen of Bishop's body. He also hadn't missed the way Bishop stared at *his* naked body, and he knew he'd made an impression. Not that it mattered—they would probably never see each other again. Thierry certainly wasn't looking forward to it. He never wanted to speak to Bishop again, and he doubted that Bishop would apologize for calling him a chicken. As far as Bishop was concerned, it was what Thierry was. The man was an asshole . . . and ignorant. It wasn't surprising that he didn't know the difference between a chicken and a French hen.

Thierry was grateful when his phone rang. He needed a distraction. That was, he was grateful until he saw who was calling. Once he did, he groaned and pulled the blanket closer to his body.

His mother would call him back if he didn't answer. That was the only reason he grabbed for his phone on the coffee table. "Maman."

"Thierry, I wasn't sure you would answer. I already called earlier, and you didn't."

"I'm sorry. I was outside in my hen form. What can I do for you?" Even though Thierry hadn't been looking forward to talking to his mother, he loved her, and he didn't want her to worry. He should have brought his phone with him outside, but he hadn't thought he would stay there for long. It was too cold.

"I just wanted to be sure you would be coming home for Christmas."

"I wouldn't miss it for anything in the world." He was looking forward to it. He saw his parents often, but there was nothing like Christmas.

"Good. Will you be bringing someone with you?"

He almost groaned again. "Maman," he whined.

"I just want you to be happy, and I truly think that having a boyfriend would help. And if you don't have one right now, the son of one of my friends is available. He just broke up with his longtime boyfriend, and he's a doctor. He would be perfect for you."

"I don't want to meet him." She always tried to set Thierry up with one or other of her friends' sons, so much so that Thierry couldn't help but wonder how many friends she had, and more importantly, how many gay sons those friends had.

"I can't help but think about you all alone in that house. It's not good for you. You need a family."

"I have a family. I have you and Papa."

"Why don't you want children? I meant that kind of family, and you know it."

Thierry had never thought about having children. He couldn't imagine himself as a father. Besides, he was single, and he had been for a while. It didn't make sense to start thinking about that kind of stuff right now. "I'm still young."

"For now, of course. You won't be young forever, though."

"And now you're making me feel old," he grumbled. He was only thirty-two, and that was *not* old.

"I want you to meet someone and be happy. As happy as I am with your father."

Thierry doubted that would happen. His parents had a once-in-a-lifetime kind of relationship. They'd fallen in love more than thirty years ago, and their feelings hadn't changed since then. They were still as much in love as ever, and Thierry knew it was an unattainable goal to have. Even if he was lucky enough to meet someone and fall in love with them, he doubted he would ever have what his parents had.

"I'll tell him to come for Christmas," his mother said. "Even if you don't think it can work, it won't hurt if you meet him."

"I can't meet him. I already have a boyfriend," Thierry said.

He regretted the words as soon as they were out of his mouth.

There was a moment of silence. Then his mother asked, "You do?"

"I do." There was no getting out of this situation now. He could tell his mother he'd lied, and she'd invite whoever she was trying to push him toward again. The last thing Thierry wanted for Christmas was to have to spend time with a guy he didn't know.

"You should have told me sooner. I wouldn't even have told you about this boy. Tell me about your boyfriend. What's his name? Where did you meet? How long have you been together? Why haven't you told me about him?"

Thierry couldn't help but chuckle. "I can't tell you anything if you don't allow me to speak."

"You're right. Come on. I'm listening. I want to know everything there is to know about him."

"His name is Bishop." Once again, Thierry regretted the words as soon as they passed his lips. What was he thinking? The only reason he could find for giving his mother that name was that Bishop had been in his yard and his thoughts only a few minutes ago. That had to be why he was still thinking about the man.

"That's a strong name. Is he a strong man?"

Thierry closed his eyes and thought about Bishop. "He is. He's taller and more muscular than me, and so gorgeous. He's also sweet. He has a niece, and she's adorable."

"Is he a shifter?"

"He's a fox shifter."

Thierry's mom clicked her tongue. "And you're sure you want to have a relationship with a fox?"

"We're not our animals, Maman. Besides, even though we're dating, it's not like we're planning on getting married anytime soon."

"Still. I want to meet him. I have to make sure he's good

enough for my son."

"Of course." Thierry was going to have to find a way to fake break up his fake relationship with Bishop before Christmas came around, and he would. In the meantime, though, it felt good to hear how happy his mom was. He felt slightly guilty for lying to her, but it would give him a few weeks of respite. It was what he needed to find a way to break up with Bishop. His mom would be sad, but he would reassure her that he and Bishop hadn't been together long.

Still, he wished he hadn't blurted out those words. He hated hurting his mother, even though she was always pushing guys in his path. She loved him, and she wanted the best for him. That was the only reason she did it. It was annoying, but he didn't truly mind, or rather, he hadn't until now.

Chapter Three

Thierry's eyes widened when he saw the smoke coming out of the engine of his car. This was the last thing he needed, and he slammed his hands on the steering wheel. "Come on, please. You can't break down right now. I need you."

Of course, his car would have none of that. The engine sputtered and died, and the only thing he could do was steer it toward the side of the road while it was still moving.

The *empty* road. The road where he hadn't seen anyone in the past ten minutes. That didn't mean no one would pass by, but it was starting to snow, and it was cold. It was also getting late. People were at home, warm, with their families, while Thierry was alone on the side of the road in his broken-down car that didn't want to start again no matter how many times he tried.

He sighed and rubbed his face with both his hands. What now? He didn't have a lot of choices. He had to call someone to pick him up, and the first person that came to mind was his mother. He wasn't about to do that, though. She was still gushing about Thierry's boyfriend and asking if Thierry would be bringing him home for Christmas, and Thierry hadn't been able to give her an answer. He didn't want to say no so she wouldn't realize something was up with Thierry's nonexistent boyfriend, but if he said yes, he might have to actually take Bishop home, something he obviously couldn't do, since they hadn't spoken since the day they'd met. He was still hoping he would be able to find a good excuse to tell his mom that he and Bishop had broken up before Christmas, but he knew that would make things even worse for her. She would gush all over Thierry, trying to make him feel better even though he didn't need it, and he would feel even guiltier. He would have to find a solution, but now wasn't the moment. He had a more pressing problem, and he didn't know what to do.

So calling his mom was out. What was left? Since he was already a customer of the only mechanic in town, he decided to call him. He wasn't sure anyone would answer, since it was already late, but to his surprise, someone did.

"Pierce and Son mechanic."

Thierry cleared his throat. "Yes, hello. My name is Thierry Leblanc. I'm sorry to disturb you right now, but my car just stopped on the side of the road, and I don't know what to do."

"You want me to send someone to pick up the car?"

"And me, please. I don't have another way home."

There was a pause before the man answered, "Well, you can come back with your car. I'll take a quick look at it and tell you if it's an easy fix or not."

With Thierry's luck, it wouldn't be. That was just how things went in his life, and he fully expected his car to be good only to be sold for parts or something like that.

He sighed again. "Please. Send someone. I'll be waiting here."

He gave the mechanic instructions where to find him, then hung up and waited. He didn't know what to do now. He hoped his car would be fixable, but he didn't have much faith in that. Since when was he lucky? He'd been pushing the car too hard, too much, for too long. The mechanic had told him the last time that he should get ready to let it go, but Thierry hadn't been, and he still wasn't. He needed the car to continue working for at least a little while.

Apparently, it wouldn't.

Thierry was relieved when he looked up and saw the

mechanic arriving. He would tow the car to the garage, and Thierry would go with him. He would be warm for at least a bit, and he would have more time to decide what was next.

Calling his mother, probably. There was no one else Thierry could call. He might as well wrap his mind around it and get used to that fact.

He hopped out of the car when the mechanic parked the truck next to it. He wished he hadn't when he saw who climbed out of it, though.

"You," he said, sounding like the hero in a bad movie.

Bishop blinked. "Hey. Your car broke down?"

Thierry snorted. "How did you guess?"

"Well, my boss sent me here, and your car is on the side of the road."

Thierry shook his head. "You don't understand sarcasm, do you?"

Bishop glared at him. "I might be a mechanic, but it doesn't mean I'm an idiot."

"You don't act like it. You keep calling me a chicken when I'm not."

"I know what I saw. You're a chicken. You might be a fancy kind of chicken, but that doesn't change what you are."

Thierry opened his mouth to tell Bishop to fuck off, but he couldn't, not if he wanted to get home tonight. Bishop was the one who held Thierry's safety in his hands and his tow truck. Without him, Thierry didn't know what he would do. Probably sleep in his car, which wasn't the best idea, considering it was snowing.

Instead of snapping back, he cleared his throat. "Will you tow my car way, please?"

"It's what I'm here for." Bishop hesitated. "I'm sorry about the fact that I keep calling you a chicken."

Thierry snorted. "You're not sorry. You just don't want me to report this to your boss." Thierry wasn't a hundred percent sure that was the case, but he wasn't willing to give in, not yet, maybe not ever when it came to Bishop.

Bishop was messing things up again, and he had to stop. It was obvious that for Thierry, the chicken thing was a sensitive issue, and Bishop had to remember that. He also had to apologize, something he should have done right from the beginning.

He sucked in a breath, then decided just to say it and mean it this time. "I'm sorry," he repeated since Thierry hadn't believed him the first time.

Thierry frowned, still staring at Bishop. "What are you sorry about? Having to rescue me?"

Bishop barely stopped himself from rolling his eyes. "No. I'm sorry if I keep calling you a chicken. I know you're not." Even though to Bishop, it looked like he was, he wasn't going to argue any more than he already had.

Thierry's eyes narrowed. "You still think I'm a chicken, don't you?"

Bishop didn't know how to answer. He didn't want to lie, especially not since Thierry was now a client, but he also didn't want to sound rude and possibly lose business. It wouldn't make the best impression on his boss. "I'll admit that I don't know the difference between normal chickens and French hens," he settled on.

Thierry started at him for a moment. He clearly wasn't happy with Bishop, and Bishop had no idea what to do with that. He'd apologized, and when Thierry had pushed, he'd explained his problem with the situation. Maybe he hadn't explained himself well enough. "I won't call you a chicken again, if that's what you're thinking. I might not understand the difference, but I'll respect your wishes. I wasn't doing it on purpose, not entirely."

Thierry snorted. "You could have fooled me."

Okay, so maybe, in the beginning, it *had* been on purpose. Bishop had found the way Thierry reacted to the chicken thing adorable. He'd been offended, and an offended Thierry was cute. Bishop was done with that, though. "I apologize," he said again. "I can't do anything more. Do you want me to call someone else?"

Thierry sighed and looked at his car. "No. It's late. I'll have to do with you."

He sounded even grumpier now, but at least he wasn't calling Bishop's boss to tell him what was going on, which was a relief. Bishop needed his job. He needed the money to take care of Carly and Ivy, no matter what Ivy said. Besides, he had rent to pay, even though he didn't spend much time in his apartment.

He turned to Thierry and nodded. "Why don't you open the hood? I'll see what's going on."

Thierry popped open the hood, and a cloud of smoke hit Bishop in the face. That wasn't good. His eyes burned and he coughed, taking a step back. "I don't think I'm going to be able to help right now. I need to tow you."

"I already knew that. It's why I called you. Well, it's why I called Mr. Pierce."

He looked like he wouldn't have called if he'd known Bishop worked there, and Bishop wasn't surprised. "You can ride with me."

Thierry looked around as if he was about to say no, but he knew as well as Bishop did that no one else would come around. If he wanted a ride home, he was going to have to accept Bishop's offer.

Thierry sighed heavily. "Fine. I'll ride with you."

He was still tense, and Bishop focused on hooking his car to the tow truck. He was used to doing this, so it didn't take him long, but even so, he regretted not telling Thierry to wait inside the truck. By the time Bishop was done, Thierry appeared half-frozen, and Bishop wished he could warm him up—possibly with his body.

Instead of offering Thierry that option and having Thierry tear him a new one, he climbed into the truck, Thierry right behind him. Bishop put the heat on, smiling when Thierry groaned in relief and held his hands close to the vent. He didn't say anything, and Bishop got them on the road. The sooner they got to the shop, the better it would be.

He'd apologized. He didn't know what else he could say to make Thierry forgive him. Maybe nothing. After all, Thierry had been attacked by Bishop's niece, and then Bishop had made fun of him. Who would want any kind of relationship with a man he met that way?

"I accept your apology," Thierry murmured.

Bishop thought he'd heard it wrong until he quickly looked at Thierry. Thierry was staring out of the windshield, but there was a tiny smile curling the corner of his lips.

Bishop couldn't help it—he grinned. "Thank you. I truly didn't mean anything bad by it. And I apologize for my niece. She shouldn't have entered your territory, and she shouldn't have attacked you."

"Don't worry about her. She's just a child. You should be careful, though. She was lucky she stumbled onto me. The other neighbors are human, as far as I know."

That was good to know, and it made Bishop realize just how lucky they'd been. "Both her mother and I talked to her. I think she knows she can't do that again. She keeps asking about you, though."

Thierry blinked. "She does?"

"You made quite an impression on her. I told her I'd ask you if she could visit, but of course, it's not like I could call you." And he hadn't outright asked if Carly could visit, even though Thierry was in the car with him. He knew better. If it was going to happen, Thierry would have to take that step, not Bishop, and not Carly.

After a moment of silence that made Bishop think the answer would be no, Thierry nodded. "She can come over. Just not through the hedge, please? I don't want to have to fix it again. She can call or even walk around the house and knock on the front door."

It was more than Bishop had expected, and he nodded happily. "So, you said you're a French hen shifter. What kind of . . . bird is that?"

Thierry looked suspicious. "Why are you asking?"

"Because I'd like to know."

Thierry didn't look convinced, but he still answered, albeit begrudgingly. "Fine. You were right. I *am* a breed of chicken. Faverolles were developed in the 1860s in France. Nowadays, we're used mostly for exhibition, but it wasn't always that way."

He stared at Bishop, and Bishop did his best not to laugh. He hadn't expected Thierry to admit he was a chicken, and he wasn't about to push his luck. "Interesting."

Thierry blinked. "Really?"

"Yes. I'm just a boring fox shifter, nothing to write home about."

"I don't think there's anything boring about you," Thierry murmured.

As soon as they were back to the shop, Thierry hopped out of the truck and looked around. His gaze stopped on Bishop's boss, and he waved. "I'm back," he said.

Pierce shook his head. "I can see that. You shouldn't be driving a piece of shit."

Thierry scowled, but it wasn't as fierce as it had been when he'd been scowling at Bishop. "How do you suggest I get around?"

"You should buy a new car."

"Are you going to buy it for me?"

Pierce huffed. Bishop could see the two were friendly, so he didn't intervene. Instead, he went about unhooking Thierry's car from the truck. He was so busy working that he didn't even notice when Pierce called him. He blinked, only to see Thierry and Pierce staring at him.

"What?" he asked.

"I said that Thierry can't go home in his car, not tonight, and obviously, I can't abandon him on the streets."

Bishop slowly nodded, unsure where this was headed. "I'm sure he can get an *Uber*."

Pierce snorted. "And put himself in the hands of someone he doesn't know? I don't think so. You can give him a ride home."

Bishop's eyes widened and he looked at Thierry, who looked just as shocked.

"He doesn't need to do that," Thierry hurriedly said.

"I don't see why he shouldn't. Unless you live out of the way?"

"I live in town, but—"

"It's decided, then. Bishop will give you a ride home. I don't know how long it's going to take for me to work on the car, though. I have to warn you, with the holidays and every-thing, it could be a week, maybe more."

Thierry groaned. "A week? How am I supposed to get around without a car?"

"Bishop will give you his phone number. You can call him anytime."

"He can?" Bishop asked. He didn't remember volunteering for this—because he hadn't.

Pierce glared at him, even though he wasn't angry, or at least, Bishop didn't think so. "I'll do my best to find a replacement car. In the meantime, please, Bishop, could you help him around town?"

How was Bishop supposed to say no to that?

Thierry needed to find a car and a fake boyfriend. Right now, he was okay since Bishop was giving him a ride home, but he wasn't sure how long that would last. He didn't think that Pierce's idea would work, not in the long term. There was no way he could call Bishop every time he needed a ride somewhere.

The fake boyfriend thing, on the other hand, might just work.

Thierry bit his lower lip. Bishop was chatting, and he didn't seem to care that Thierry was barely listening to him. Unless he hadn't noticed, which was also a possibility. Thierry didn't think so, though. Bishop struck him as the kind of person who knew everything that was happening around him, even though he didn't seem to.

That had nothing to do with Thierry's problems, though, and he went back to them.

Bishop could be his fake boyfriend. He'd told his mom Bishop was his boyfriend, and it would be the easiest way out of this. Well, the easiest way would be to tell his mom that he and Bishop had broken up just before Christmas, but then she would look at him with pity in her eyes the entire time he was there. He didn't want that. He didn't deserve it, not when he was a lying liar who lied.

That was what he had to do, though. Bishop was a nice guy, even though he still thought of Thierry as a chicken — and as Thierry had reluctantly admitted, he wasn't wrong — and while he'd been initially rude, he wasn't anymore. He'd apologized more times than he'd needed to, and Thierry knew he wouldn't make that mistake again. He might still think Thierry was a chicken, but he wouldn't tell him to his face.

The problems started once they reached Thierry's home. Well, *more* problems started. Thierry's mom was at his front door, and she beamed when she noticed Bishop and Thierry in Bishop's car.

"I forgot my mom was coming over for dinner," Thierry explained. He sounded calm, but inside, he was freaking out. He hated disappointing his mom. He hadn't wanted to lie. She would probably understand if he explained. She was his mom.

"She looks nice," Bishop said, peering through the windshield.

Thierry's mom waved at him, grinning. Bishop looked from Thierry's mom to Thierry, then back at her before waving as if it was perfectly normal for him to do so.

Thierry rolled his eyes. "You're encouraging her."

"I just waved hello. You expected me to ignore her?"

He hadn't. Bishop wasn't the kind of person who ignored people. That didn't solve Thierry's problem, though. He couldn't ask Bishop to fake date him, could he?

He had to, though, because his mom was coming toward the car, and he wouldn't be able to lie to her face, not with Bishop right next to her. He couldn't tell Bishop to run while he still had time, either, not when Bishop was grinning like a loon.

"Thierry!" his mother exclaimed as he got out of the car.

He wasn't planning on introducing Bishop, and he hoped she would forgive him for being so rude. "I'm sorry, I forgot we were supposed to have dinner together," he rushed to say, hoping Bishop would take the opportunity to leave.

His mom looked behind him at Bishop, who, for some reason, was stepping out of the car, too. "Don't apologize. If I'd know you were seeing your boyfriend tonight, I would have told you we didn't have to see each other."

Bishop had heard. He had to, considering how close he was

to Thierry's mom. There was no way around it. Thierry had to find a way to ask Bishop's to be his fake boyfriend, and he had to do it right now.

Bishop's eyes were wide. He opened his mouth, possibly to tell Thierry's mom she was mistaken, but Thierry moved closer and took one of Bishop's hands, squeezing until it hurt. "I thought I would be here sooner. We lost track of time. Sorry."

His mom was still beaming, while Thierry prayed Bishop would understand and that he'd go along with it. Thierry didn't know what he would do otherwise.

Bishop frowned at him, and Thierry blinked, hoping to silently tell him to go along with what he was saying.

"It's a pleasure to meet you, Bishop," his mom said, revealing the fact that Thierry had talked to her about Bishop.

Thierry wanted the earth to open under him and swallow him, but unfortunately, it didn't.

Bishop extracted his hand from Thierry's and shook his mom's hand. "It's a pleasure to meet you, ma'am."

"And so polite. I'm delighted Thierry found a nice man. It was about time."

Bishop turned his attention back to Thierry. "I'm not sure he shares that opinion, but I'm happy I found him, too."

Thierry almost hugged him in relief. Bishop clearly had no idea what was going on, but he was going along with the fake boyfriend story, and that was all Thierry cared about right now.

"Why would he think you're not polite?" Thierry's mom asked.

Thierry shook his head. "Only because the first time we met, he was rude. He called me a chicken. Why don't we go inside, Maman? It's cold."

"Of course," Thierry's mom turned to Bishop. "I know it wasn't planned, but you can stay with us for dinner if you want. And don't worry when it comes to the food. There'll be more than enough for the three of us."

Thierry hadn't thought it possible, but Bishop's smile became even wider—and wicked. "I'd be happy to have dinner with you."

This was it. Thierry was going to die.

Thierry was angry, and Bishop didn't care. That would teach him to tell his mother that Bishop was his boyfriend even though it wasn't true and they hated each other.

Well, Thierry hated Bishop. Bishop certainly didn't hate Thierry, and he knew it was his fault that Thierry felt that way toward him. *Still.* He hadn't even thought to mention this to Bishop, and Bishop felt like he was owed a little revenge, so he grinned at Thierry's mother.

"I have to admit, I was surprised when Thierry told me he had a boyfriend," she said as she hooked her arm around Bishop's and dragged him toward Thierry's front door.

Bishop turned around and winked at Thierry, who was standing still, staring at them. That seemed to jostle him into moving, and he glared at Bishop as he strode toward the door.

He slipped, barely managing to stay on his feet. Bishop barked out a laugh, and if Thierry's looks could have killed, Bishop would probably already be buried under the snow.

"What can I say? I'm special that way," he told Thierry's mother, turning to her again. "I'm at a disadvantage, though. You know about me, but I don't even know your name."

She turned to Thierry and arched a brow at him. He looked away, which made Bishop's smile widen. No adult should be adorable, but Bishop had thought Thierry was since the beginning, and nothing he'd seen since then had made him change his mind.

Thierry's mom beamed at Bishop. "You can call me Maman

like Thierry does—it means mom—or Anne. And I'm happy to meet you. Now, tell me, what are you doing for Christmas?"

Bishop heard Thierry suck in a breath, but he ignored him. He knew where this was going, and while he wished he could say yes to Thierry's mom, he doubted that would go down well with his *boyfriend*. "I'm spending Christmas with my sister and my niece. They live next door, actually." He pointed at Ivy's house.

Anne—there was no way Bishop would call her *Maman*—appeared delighted. "Is that how the two of you met? Thierry mentioned it, but since he's been hiding you, I'm sure he kept some things from me."

"It is. My niece escaped the yard and snuck into his. I went after her, and the rest is history."

"She tried to eat me," Thierry grumbled as he opened the door.

"I'm sure you're exaggerating," Anne told him. She turned to look at Bishop. "He's that kind of guy, always so dramatic."

It was hard not to laugh, but Bishop nodded. He knew he could talk freely with Thierry's mom about Thierry being a shifter because he had to have taken after her or his father. Either way, she had to know. "Carly is only five, and she enjoys running around in her shifted form."

"Thierry did mention you were a shifter."

"I'm a fox."

Anne's smile was wicked. "You're a fox shifter, and Thierry is a French hen."

"I won't eat him, though. Don't worry." Bishop only realized the double meaning of his words when Thierry's mother blushed. Luckily for him, it was time for them to follow Thierry inside.

He was nowhere to be seen, having abandoned his jacket and boots in the entrance. Bishop could hear him stomping around, though, and he knew Thierry wouldn't be happy.

He didn't care.

He was hungry, and if he was honest with himself, he was curious about Thierry. He wanted to know more about him, and he knew asking Thierry wouldn't help. Asking Thierry's mother, on the other hand, would.

"Thierry and I haven't been together long, just a few weeks," he told her.

"Maybe that's why he didn't tell us about you sooner."

Bishop reached out and helped her out of her jacket. Her cheeks were still red, and she looked flustered. He grinned at her, hoping it meant she liked him. He and Thierry weren't together, but he couldn't deny the thought was appealing.

That was, if he wanted to risk being killed in his sleep. With the way Thierry was glaring at him and slamming things around, it was a distinct possibility.

"You said your niece was playing in her fox form?" Anne asked as they headed toward what had to be the kitchen if the sound of pots and pans being banged together was an indication.

"She was. She's still learning that she has to be careful when she shifts, and of course, that she shouldn't be sneaking into neighbors yards. I think that she was just looking around and noticed Thierry in his French hen form. She was intrigued, and she acted on instinct."

"Well, that's understandable. Once, when Thierry was four, he ran away. We found him with the neighbors' chickens in the henhouse. One of them had taken him under her wing, and quite literally. She wasn't happy when I got him back. It took the bite marks a few days to disappear."

"Maman!" Thierry yelled. "Don't tell him that."

Anne put her hands on her hips. "And why not? He's your boyfriend."

Bishop grinned at Thierry. "Exactly. I'm your boyfriend. I

should know these things. You stayed with the chickens, then?"

Thierry glared so hard at Bishop that he was surprised not to find a hole in his forehead. "It's none of your business. Stop talking to my mother."

"Thierry, why are you so rude to your boyfriend?" Anne asked. "You weren't fighting when you got here, were you?"

"Of course not, Anne. We're still in the honeymoon phase," Bishop told her.

He was having a great time, and he knew it wasn't over yet. He moved closer to Thierry, wrapping an arm around his waist and kissing the top of his head. Thierry stiffened against him, but Bishop didn't move. Thierry had told his mother they were boyfriends, so he was going to act like it unless he wanted Bishop to tell his mother the truth. It might be cruel, but so was using Bishop as a fake boyfriend without telling him about it. What if Bishop had a boyfriend already?

Anne's expression softened when she saw Bishop and Thierry together. Bishop couldn't stop smiling. "Thierry loves me. He also loves to insult me, though," he said.

"He shouldn't. If he wants you to stay with him, he should be nice."

"Because Bishop has no other reason to stay with me?" Thierry asked, sounding like he might bang Bishop over the head with his pan if he gave the wrong answer.

Bishop decided to back off, at least for a bit. The last thing he wanted was to be teasing Thierry while Thierry had a knife in his hands. So, instead of continuing prodding him, he stepped back and headed to the counter. He was pretty sure there was nothing he could do, but he still offered. "What can I do?"

Of course, Anne turned him down and ordered him to sit down. "You're a guest. We're not going to make you work."

Bishop obeyed. He relaxed as he listened to Anne and

Thierry talk. He hadn't talked to his mom in a long time, and he missed that. It made his heart ache, and especially because he knew Thierry was trying to make Anne happy. Bishop didn't know why Thierry had told his mom that he had a boyfriend even though he didn't, but he suspected it was to make her happy. Bishop understood that. He didn't have a mother to keep happy anymore, and he wished he did.

He knew that if he said anything, though, Thierry would tell him to go to hell. It was just the kind of relationship they had—the real one, not the fake one.

"So, Bishop, you said you were going to spend Christmas with your sister and your niece?" Anne asked as she chopped tomatoes and onions.

"That's right."

"What about your parents? Won't they be there?"

The usual flare of pain constricted Bishop's chest. He'd learned to ignore it, though, and to push through it. "They died several years ago. A car accident. There're only the three of us left."

Her expression shifted to sadness. "I'm sorry."

"Don't worry about it. You didn't know."

"Still. I should be more careful about how I talk to people. I don't like the thought of you, your sister, and your niece all alone for Christmas, though. Why don't you come over? Thierry's father would be happy to meet you, and I'd love to have a big family Christmas."

Thierry dropped the tongs he was using to poke at the steaks in his pan. "He already told you he had plans, Maman."

She shrugged. "So? It's still a few weeks away, and I'm sure that whatever food they already bought can be kept for longer. Did you have anything special planned?"

"We didn't. Just dinner at home, the three of us."

Bishop knew this was going to be a problem, though. He

wanted to say yes to Thierry's mom. He wanted to continue teasing him, but more importantly, he wanted to give Ivy and Carly a family Christmas. He could already tell right away that Anne would treat them as if they were part of the family. That was something Bishop missed and that Carly had never known, and Bishop wanted to give her that at least once.

Maybe he could.

"I'd be delighted to come," he told Anne, carefully avoiding to look at Thierry. He was pretty sure that if he did, he would find smoke coming out of his ears. "I'll ask Ivy and Carly, of course, but it won't be a problem."

Anne beamed. "I'm so happy to hear that. It's the first time for Thierry to bring home a boyfriend, and I can't wait to meet your niece. She sounds so sweet."

"She is, but she's also a troublemaker. Let me tell you what happened when she was three. She met this dog, and—" Bishop had no idea what he was doing in this situation, but he knew he *was* doing it, Thierry be damned.

CHAPTER FOUR

Thierry was going to kill Bishop. He would have to wait until his mother left, of course, but he thought he could do it before the end of the evening. It was a pity that Carly would never see her uncle again, but Thierry couldn't let this slide.

Why had Bishop agreed to come over for Christmas? Thierry knew how hard it would have been to resist, but Bishop could have said no, even though Thierry's mom could guilt even the most innocent man into doing whatever she wanted.

Still. Bishop *should* have said no. He should have found an excuse not to come. What were the two of them supposed to do? Play boyfriends over Christmas? Thierry didn't think he could do it, especially since now he would have to lie to four people instead of two.

But mostly because he wasn't sure he could resist Bishop's charms for that long.

He huffed and stabbed his fork into a piece of meat. He didn't know what to do. He wanted to keep his mom happy, and right now, she was. Bishop seemed to be the perfect boyfriend for Thierry, except for the fact that he'd been rude and had kept insulting him until today, and of course, because they weren't actually together.

"What's going on with you?" Thierry's mom asked. "Did your steak insult you? You're stabbing it as if you hate it."

Thierry narrowed his eyes, but he couldn't glare at her. "I'm just starving."

"It's a good thing I brought dessert, then. You already ate all the food on your plate. I'll go get it, or maybe you want more salad or vegetables?"

"Sit down, Maman. I'm fine." Thierry was *not* hungry, not after rage-eating all the food on his plate. It had been easier to focus on the food than on Bishop and the conversation he was having with Thierry's mom.

"Yes, sit down." Bishop got to his feet. "Thierry and I will clean up. Don't worry about a thing."

"I can't leave the two of you to do all the work," Thierry's mom tried to protest.

Thierry wasn't surprised. She liked having everything under control and for it to be done the way she wanted it done.

"Really, Anne. Sit. You worked hard to cook us dinner. The least we can do is clean up."

Thierry wanted to point out that Bishop hadn't done anything while he'd help cook, but he didn't. Instead, he got to his feet, grabbed his plate, and rushed to the kitchen. He needed a second to breathe. He needed some time away from Bishop so he could gather his thoughts.

But Bishop was right behind him, and while they couldn't exactly have a conversation with Thierry's mom right next door, Thierry needed to say something. "Why did you agree to come over for Christmas?" he hissed.

"What did you want me to do?"

"You could have said no."

"How was I supposed to do that? She clearly wants me, my sister, and my niece to come."

"She does, but it's not going to happen. You have to tell her that you have something else to do, or you know what? Why don't you actually *plan* something else? That way, it won't be a lie anymore."

Bishop briefly looked toward the dining room. "I can't do that to your mom."

"She'll be sad, but she'll understand. Christmas is about family."

"Exactly, and Ivy and Carly currently don't have a family. This might be the only chance to see what a real Christmas is like. I won't take that away from them, not now that I can give it to them."

Thierry blinked. Bishop had mentioned that his parents had died in a car accident, but Thierry hadn't thought much about it. Surely, Bishop and his sister had more family. Thierry had a number of aunts and uncles and too many cousins for one person to have. He'd thought the same would go for Bishop, but from the sound of it, that wasn't the case. "It's really only going to be the three of you for Christmas?" he asked.

Bishop nodded curtly. "It is. If it was just me, I would tell your mother I can't come. I know you don't want me there, and I promise you I will try to stay as far away from you as I can. I have to come, though. I have to give Ivy and Carly this chance."

"I don't want you to think that you're obligated." Thierry sucked in a breath. He understood where Bishop was coming from now, and for whatever reason, he wanted Carly to have a good Christmas. He also had to say something about the way Bishop had handled the fake boyfriend situation. "Thank you for going along with this. I told my mom you were my boyfriend because she kept trying to fix me up with other guys. She was going to invite one of them over for Christmas, and I didn't want her to. I told her I already had a boyfriend, and when she asked for more details, I panicked."

"And you told her *I* was your boyfriend." Bishop sounded satisfied.

Thierry didn't like it, but there wasn't much he could do. Bishop was doing him a huge favor. The least he could do was agree to have Bishop and his family over for Christmas. "You can come. I just didn't want you to think that you had to."

"Don't worry about me. I want my sister and my niece to be happy at Christmas. That's all. I'll stay away from you, and you can break-up with me the next day if that's what you want."

"Boys?" Thierry's mom called from the dining room. "You need help in there?"

Thierry poked his head of the door so she could see him. "Don't worry about us, Maman. We're okay."

She beamed at him, and Thierry couldn't remember the last time he'd seen her so happy. He despised the fact that she was happy because of a lie, but there was nothing he could do right now. He didn't want to hurt her even more by telling her he'd lied.

"I bet I can guess what you two are doing in there," she said, still smiling. "You know, you can kiss him even though I'm there. I won't mind. I was young, once, too, and I still love your father as much as I did back then."

Thierry groaned. "I know that. I caught you and Papa enough times to be aware of the fact that you're still in love. And we weren't kissing. We were just talking about Christmas."

Thierry's mom's smile softened. "I'm glad they'll come. Their story is so sad, and I can't believe the three of them would have been alone for Christmas otherwise. I'm happy you found him, Thierry. He's good for you, but I think you'll be good for him, too."

Thierry wasn't too sure about that, but he'd started this farce, and he would have to finish it — with Bishop of all people.

Even though Bishop hadn't had a problem faking being Thierry's boyfriend, he was relieved when Thierry's mom left.

He could have done without the wink she sent him, though, because he suspected she thought he was staying around and taking her son to bed. It made him uncomfortable, but he laughed it off.

He breathed more easily once the door was closed. He and Thierry had had a hushed conversation in the kitchen, and he knew they needed to talk more. They'd been interrupted, and that didn't make for the best conversations, especially not in the situation they were in.

Thierry was still rinsing the dishes when Bishop got back to the kitchen. He watched him for a while, wondering what to do.

He knew he was the reason they'd started their relation-ship—if it could even be called a relationship—on the wrong foot. He shouldn't have talked to Thierry the way he had, and more importantly, he shouldn't have called him a chicken, since that seemed to be a sore spot for Thierry. He'd apolo-gized, but it was obvious by now that Thierry didn't like him very much. Which was why the fact that he'd told his mom he and Bishop were dating didn't make sense. Why was Bishop the first person who had come to mind?

Bishop wanted answers, but he doubted he would get them. Thierry struck him as a private person and as someone who didn't like explaining himself.

"What do you want me to do?" he asked.

Thierry jerked as if he hadn't heard Bishop, and maybe he hadn't. He'd been lost in his thoughts, and Bishop felt sorry for disturbing him.

"I thought you'd left with my mom," he said as he reached for a towel to dry his hands.

"I think staying was the best thing to do. She currently thinks I'm going to stay the night. I would have had to explain why I didn't if I'd left with her."

Thierry grimaced. "Right. She thinks you're staying

because you're my boyfriend."

"Exactly." Bishop crossed his arms over his chest and leaned his hip against the counter.

He was surprised when he noticed that Thierry was staring at his biceps, but he didn't say anything about it. The worst thing he could do right now was to tease Thierry. They'd just reached what felt like a truce. He didn't want to make Thierry angry.

Bishop cleared his throat. "So, Christmas."

Thierry sighed. He hung the towel and turned to face Bishop, and Bishop half expected him to yell. Thierry didn't want Bishop to spend Christmas with his family, and Bishop understood why. He'd acted impulsively earlier, telling Thierry that he was coming whether or not he wanted him to, but he realized now how stupid that was. Yes, he wanted to give Ivy and Carly a Christmas with family, but Thierry's family wasn't theirs. They would be guests, nothing more. Thierry, on the other hand, would be at home, and he would be uncomfortable because of them. Bishop didn't want that to happen, and he knew that Ivy would kick his ass if she found out about this.

"Well, I can't say that I'm particularly happy that you and your family will be over for Christmas," Thierry said.

Bishop swallowed. "I know I told your mom we'd be there, and I told you I wanted to come, but I shouldn't have. It's stupid. They're your family, not mine, and you deserve to be relaxed and comfortable on Christmas. We'll stay home. You're going to have to find a way to tell your family we're not coming, though. Your mom won't be happy, although if you wait until the last possible moment to tell her, she probably won't be able to do anything about it."

Thierry grimaced. "As long as she doesn't invite anyone else to set me up with."

"You could just tell her we're still together and that Carly got sick. That way she'll think we're still a couple until after Christmas. Then, you can decide to tell her we broke up." Of course, he would have New Year's to worry about, but that wasn't Bishop's problem.

Thierry bit his lower lip, and Bishop found himself taking a step closer to him. He hadn't thought much about it, not given the way they'd been fighting since the moment they met, but he kind of liked Thierry, even though he'd tried to convince himself otherwise. He liked that Thierry wanted to make his mom happy. He liked that he was strong headed, convinced of his worth, and that he stood up for himself. He also liked the way Thierry looked, of course. It might be stupid, since they were fox and French hen, but Bishop didn't think it mattered.

He wanted to kiss Thierry.

Doing so would bring a set of complications that Thierry probably didn't want to deal with. He and Thierry were fake boyfriends, but that didn't mean they had to kiss. Bishop *wanted* to kiss Thierry, though. He wanted to feel his plump lips against his, to check if Thierry tasted of the dessert they'd eaten earlier. He wanted to see if it would mellow him, if he'd be a bit happier and less grumpy after he was kissed senseless—and if he *could* kiss Thierry senseless.

He moved even closer, reaching for Thierry. He saw the way Thierry's eyes widened, but he didn't pause. He was sure that if Thierry didn't want to do this, he would find a way to let Bishop know—probably by punching him on the nose or something.

Bishop hooked an arm around Thierry's waist and pulled him close. Then, before Thierry could protest, he kissed him.

Thierry froze for a second, and Bishop waited. He didn't push to deepen the kiss, not yet—not ever, if Thierry didn't want it. When Thierry didn't react, Bishop started to move away, knowing he'd made a mistake.

Then Thierry reached out, burying his hands into Bishop's hair and pulling him close. He opened his mouth, and his tongue darted out.

They were kissing.

He tasted as good as Bishop had thought he would. He was sweet from the dessert they'd eaten, but there was more to the kiss. Thierry was strong, complicated, but also fragile. There was a lot of history in Thierry, and Bishop wanted to uncover all of it.

The problem was that this was confusing for both of them.

Bishop took a step back, dropping his arms. He and Thierry stared at each other, both of them panting. Thierry looked even more gorgeous now, his lips slick with saliva, slightly reddened by the kiss. His eyes were wide, his pupils blown, and he was staring at Bishop as if he couldn't believe what Bishop had done.

Bishop couldn't, either.

"What was that for?" Thierry finally asked.

Bishop rubbed his face. "I'm sorry. I shouldn't have." He shook his head and moved away from Thierry even more. "I'm going to go. I doubt your mom is still out there, so she won't know about it." He knew he should have waited and that they should talk about the kiss and everything else, but he couldn't. Instead, he rushed to the entrance, pushing his feet into his boots, not even taking the time to lean down and tie them. He was putting his jacket on when Thierry appeared in the entrance.

Bishop looked at him. He couldn't do this. He shouldn't want to kiss Thierry, because he had to focus on Ivy and Carly. They were the only important people in Bishop's world.

Or at least, they should have been.

Thierry was *not* going to allow Bishop to run away from this, whatever *this* was. He had no idea what they were doing, why Bishop had kissed him, but he wanted answers, and he would get them.

"What are you doing?" he asked.

Bishop looked away. "I thought it was obvious. I'm going home."

"Why?"

"Because we're not really boyfriends. I don't have a reason to spend the night. Unless you think your mother will come back?"

"She won't. Why did you kiss me?"

Bishop paused, half of his jacket on, the other half hanging from his body. "I don't know."

"Why are you running, then?"

Bishop shook his head. He was hesitant, and Thierry wanted to know why. He wasn't sure why, but he didn't think it mattered, not right now. He was a mess of feelings he didn't have the time to sort through, and this was part of it.

Bishop ran a hand through his hair. "I shouldn't have kissed you."

Thierry couldn't help but think that he'd had his hands in Bishop's hair, too, only a few seconds ago. It was short but very soft, and to his own surprise, Thierry couldn't wait to bury his hands in it again. To do that, though, he would have to convince Bishop it was a good idea. He would have to convince *himself* it was a good idea.

He didn't know why he thought it was. He and Bishop went together like water and oil. They didn't mix, and they shouldn't be doing this, especially considering the fact that Thierry had told his mom that he and Bishop were an item.

But maybe they could be. Maybe they could change this from being a lie to being a reality. Even though Bishop had been rude initially and had kept calling Thierry a chicken, he'd apologized. Besides, Thierry knew himself. He was pretty touchy when it came to his animal form, mostly because everyone called him a chicken—and in the end, he was. He might not like it, but he couldn't change it, and he couldn't change the fact that most shifters thought chicken shifters were stupid. What Bishop had done wasn't a mortal offense, and clearly, it hadn't stopped Thierry from liking him.

"Come to the living room," he said softly, hoping it would entice Bishop to follow him.

"I should go home. We don't have to see each other again."

"What if I *want* to see you again?" It was a risk, but it was a risk Thierry wanted to take. He hoped it wasn't putting his heart in jeopardy, but he didn't think so. On the one hand, if Bishop told him to fuck off, it wasn't like they'd spent a lot of time together. He found Bishop attractive, and he liked the kind of man he was, but they didn't know each other.

On the other hand, if Bishop said yes, they could have something together. What, Thierry didn't know yet, but he supposed he would find out.

Bishop sighed. "This is going to complicate everything. Besides, I can't do it."

"What can't you do?"

Bishop looked at Thierry. "Have a relationship."

Thierry waited, but when Bishop didn't explain, he asked, "Why not? Are you married?"

Bishop jerked and took a step back. "Of course not. I wouldn't have kissed you if I was married."

"What is it, then? Why can't you have a relationship?" Thierry wasn't sure why he was so focused on having a possible relationship with Bishop, but he'd learned a long time ago to listen to his instincts. He wanted Bishop, and Bishop wanted him. The only problem was that something was stopping Bishop from taking what he wanted, and Thierry had to find out what it was. He couldn't work it through with Bishop if he didn't.

Bishop shook his head, but Thierry could see he was softening. He hadn't left the house yet. He still had half his jacket and his boots on, but Thierry hoped it was a sign he didn't want to go.

He reached out and gently helped Bishop out of his jacket. "Come on. Let's go sit on the couch. You can talk to me." Bishop opened his mouth, probably to remind Thierry that he couldn't have a relationship, but Thierry would have none of that. "I know, I know. You can't have a relationship. This isn't a relationship, though. It's just us talking. It's obvious that you haven't talked to anyone in a long time, so you can talk to me."

Bishop's lips quirked with a half-smile. "I thought you hated me."

Thierry looked away, but he was smiling, too. "Hate is such a strong word. I disliked you, mostly because you called me a chicken. But in the end, it's what I am. I'm a French hen, which is a kind of chicken."

Bishop burst out laughing, and Thierry hoped that meant he was staying. Sure enough, Bishop leaned down to take his boots off, and Thierry relaxed. He didn't know what was going to happen, but at least they had a chance at something, since Bishop was staying.

Bishop allowed Thierry to take one of his hands and guide him to the living room. They sat on the couch, and Thierry waited. He wanted to know what was happening, but Bishop had to explain the story. Thierry wasn't going to try to get it out of him by force. If Bishop wasn't ready to talk about it, whatever it was, he'd let it go, even though he thought they could have something good together. Why he thought that was anyone's guess, but he wasn't going to fight it.

Bishop sighed again. He looked tired, wary, and Thierry wished he could do something for him. Maybe he could. He could listen to him, give him a shoulder to cry on if that was what he needed.

"I told you and your mom that Ivy and I are alone in the world. Well, there's Carly, too, but it's just the three of us."

"Because your parents died in a car accident."

"They did. It was several years ago, and that means that I had to protect Ivy. I didn't do a good job, though. She met this guy, and he took advantage of her. He got her pregnant, then, he vanished. He left her with a baby when she was little more than a baby herself."

Thierry frowned. He hadn't met Ivy yet, but how much younger than Bishop was she to have been a baby herself when she got pregnant? Carly was five, so Ivy would have gotten pregnant about six years ago.

"How old are you?" he asked Bishop.

Bishop shook his head. "What do you care? I'm telling you what you wanted to know."

"I care because I'm trying to understand. You said that Ivy was little more than a baby when she had Carly. How old is she?"

Bishop rubbed the back of his neck. "She's twenty-five."

So she would have been around nineteen when she got pregnant. Thierry understood better where Bishop was coming from now, but not entirely. "What about you?"

"I turned thirty this year."

"And you've been taking care of her for a while."

"Our parents died when she was sixteen."

Thierry quickly counted, then sucked in a breath. "You were only twenty-one. Yet you took care of her."

"I tried. I didn't do a good job, though."

"She was an adult when she got pregnant." But Thierry didn't want to fight over this. He knew that whatever he said, it wouldn't change Bishop's mind when it came to his sister. "And more importantly, she's one now. You don't have to protect her."

Bishop jerked. "Of course I have to protect her. She's my baby sister."

Thierry raised his hands. "Okay. So you have to protect her. That doesn't mean that you don't have space for anything or anyone else in your life, though."

"I didn't do a good job before. I won't allow that to happen again."

Bishop was a good man. Thierry had felt that from the beginning, and he was sure of it now. He understood the situation better, but he thought Bishop didn't see the entire picture.

He wasn't sure he ever would, or that there would be space for Thierry or anyone else in his life.

Bishop knew what Thierry wanted, and he wanted to go along with it, desperately. He hadn't allowed himself to have a relationship in six years, ever since Ivy had gotten pregnant. He didn't think he could have one now, either. He understood what Thierry was saying—Ivy was an adult, and she didn't need him.

Except, she did. How could she not? They only had each other, and Bishop didn't mind. He was always happy to give her money if she needed it, to help her pay rent, to babysit for her. It didn't mean he didn't realize that over the years he'd lost himself, though. He was living only for Ivy and Carly, and he'd been only living for them for the past six years. Something had to break, and apparently, it would start with Thierry.

Bishop wanted to run. He didn't want to open himself up and to possibly allow himself to break the promise he'd made to himself to take care of Ivy and Carly. Thierry was a distraction, but Bishop found that he was a distraction he couldn't resist.

For once, he wanted to allow himself to take what he wanted. He wanted to feel loved in a way that wasn't sisterly. He wanted more than what he'd had for the past six years, and he knew that for a moment, Thierry would be able to give that to him.

Just for a moment, though. Bishop already knew he wouldn't be able to have a relationship with Thierry, but he allowed himself to think he could. He allowed himself to believe that this wouldn't be a one-night stand, he could have more, that he could introduce his sister to Thierry, and that they could spend Christmas together.

Instead of continuing to think, he reached out and dragged Thierry closer.

Thierry squeaked, but he yielded, and he didn't protest when Bishop pulled him into his lap. Instead, Thierry wrapped his arms around Bishop's neck and kissed him.

Bishop allowed himself to relax. For just half an hour, he wanted to forget about everything waiting for him outside of this house. He wanted to forget that he was Ivy's only support system, that if she lost him, she would be alone. He wanted to forget that it was his duty to take care of her, to focus on her, and he wanted to focus on Thierry instead.

So he did.

They were still kissing when he moved, getting to his feet, almost falling because of Thierry's weight. Thierry squeaked again and wrapped himself around Bishop, and Bishop allowed him to. They weren't going far anyway. He twisted until he could spread Thierry on his back on the couch, then he hovered over him, staring down at him.

"You're gorgeous," he murmured, aware of the reverence in his voice.

Thierry's cheeks pinked, and he looked away. "You only think that because you're about to get laid."

Bishop laughed. "It doesn't change the fact that you're

gorgeous." Even though Bishop *was* about to get laid.

He reached for Thierry's t-shirt, pushing it up until it bunched under Thierry's armpits. Thierry was slim, but muscular. Bishop spread his fingers on Thierry's stomach. He could feel the muscles moving, and he smiled. Then he leaned down, kissing Thierry's bellybutton.

Thierry sucked in a breath, but Bishop ignored him. He was smiling against Thierry's skin, and he put his mouth to good use, exploring every inch he could reach on Thierry's body as his hands worked on opening Thierry's jeans.

Thierry was already wriggling under him, and Bishop loved that he was the one making it happen. He was the one who'd pushed Thierry to admit that he actually was a chicken shifter, and more importantly, to forgive him for teasing him about it.

None of that mattered right now. Thierry was spread under Bishop, and Bishop couldn't remember ever wanting anyone the way he wanted Thierry. He could only allow himself to have this once — or maybe not. He didn't know, but he would have to make sure he didn't fall too deep into it.

That, too, was something he didn't have to worry about right now, though.

He finished unfastening Thierry's jeans and pushed them down his thighs. Thierry helped, lifting his ass, then his feet so that Bishop could slide the jeans and his underwear off his body. He was hard, his cock standing up in a nest of blond hair.

Thierry buried his fingers in Bishop's hair, gently tugging. Bishop looked up to make sure Thierry was still okay with what was happening.

Thierry looks debauched. His lips were red, as if he'd been biting on them while Bishop explored his body. His cheeks were pink, as was his chest. He looked delectable, and Bishop wanted to eat him up.

So he did.

It wasn't comfortable, since the couch was short, but Bishop managed to settle on his stomach with his legs up, folded at the knee. He swallowed Thierry's cock, ignoring the way Thierry tugged on his hair, how he undulated under him. He wanted to drive Thierry crazy so he would remember him once this was over.

He wanted to remember it, too.

He licked up and down Thierry's cock, trying to find the best way to make him come. He teased his balls, even pressed a finger behind them, massaging Thierry's hole. He was surprised when Thierry didn't say anything about it. He'd expected Thierry to want to be in control, especially in bed, but Thierry seemed to be more than happy to surrender to Bishop.

Bishop took advantage of that.

Thierry didn't say anything as Bishop moved him this way and that, as he sucked on his cock, as he fingered his ass. He let Bishop do what he wanted, panting through it, pulling on Bishop's hair, trying to make him move closer. Bishop wasn't ready for that, though, so he focused on Thierry's pleasure instead. Every time he felt that Thierry was about to come, he retreated. He stopped sucking Thierry's cock, giving him time to breathe, to come down from the high.

Thierry was unhappy with him. That much was obvious from the way he was scowling at him. Bishop was satisfied, though. If this was the only time they would have this, he wanted to make the most out of it.

When he felt like he was about to explode, he finally pushed his own jeans down. They felt restrictive, and he wanted to be skin to skin with Thierry, but he limited himself to rolling them down his thighs. Then he lowered himself on top of Thierry, kissing him. Thierry instantly wrapped himself around Bishop, holding him close, thrusting his hips up, using the hold he had around Bishop's waist to rub their cocks together. Bishop, on the other hand, pushed down.

The friction was delicious. Bishop wanted so much more of it. He wanted to make Thierry come, and he wanted to come himself. He wanted them to become one, but he knew that wasn't possible. It was too intimate, and they didn't know each other well enough for that, not yet. Thierry hadn't mentioned it, and Bishop wasn't going to, either. This was enough. It was *more* than enough. It was perfect, and when Bishop came, he screwed his eyes shut and buried his face against Thierry's neck. He inhaled Thierry's scent, basking in it, sending it to memory.

Thierry was still wrapped around him, and they both stayed still.

Bishop wanted to stay like this forever. Thierry's body had relaxed under him, and their combined releases were spreading on their stomachs, probably sticking them together already. It didn't matter. Bishop stayed right where he was, enjoying the moment.

He wanted more. He wanted *Thierry*, and for now, he had him. He found himself hoping that the moment wouldn't end with tonight. He didn't know what was next, neither for him and Thierry nor for him and Ivy, but he would find out sooner rather than later.

It terrified him.

CHAPTER FIVE

Bishop knew where he was when he woke up. He'd allowed Thierry to talk him into staying for the night, and they were still wrapped around each other, both of them naked. Thierry's head was on the pillow right next to Bishop, but he was looking the other way while Bishop hugged him from behind. Thierry was warm and solid between Bishop's arms, and Bishop kept his eyes closed, knowing that he had to get up. He didn't want this to end, though. He wanted to stay here until Thierry woke up, for them to have breakfast together, then maybe have sex again. They'd spent most of the night lost in each other, and Bishop had managed to avoid thinking about the future during that time.

He couldn't anymore.

It was already over. No matter how much he liked Thierry and wanted him in his life, he had to focus on Ivy. She was only twenty-five, and she was already a mom. She needed his help. Besides, he couldn't forget what had happened when he hadn't been taking care of her. She'd gotten pregnant after that asshole had taken advantage of her, and it could have destroyed her life. They'd worked hard, both of them, to make sure that didn't happen, but Bishop could never forget that it was his fault. He should have been a better brother. He should have kept an eye on her, protected her, and he'd failed. He'd promised himself he would never fail again, and if that meant that he couldn't have a relationship, that he could never have anyone else to focus on in his life, then so be it.

He opened his eyes.

Thierry's blond hair was spread on the pillow. It smelled of coconut, and Bishop wanted to bury his face against it. He resisted the urge. He had to get out of bed before Thierry woke up. He didn't want them to talk about what was next. He'd been clear yesterday that he couldn't have a relationship, but he suspected Thierry thought he could change his mind.

He couldn't. No matter how much Bishop wanted it, no matter how much he'd enjoyed himself last night, no matter how much he wanted him and Thierry to have something, he *couldn't* give in.

Luckily for him, he had a lot of experience sneaking out of bedrooms. In the first years after his parents died, he and Ivy had shared an apartment. She was a light sleeper, especially after Carly was born, and Bishop had learned to be quiet as a ghost in the morning so he wouldn't wake either of them. It came in handy today, and he managed to sneak out of bed and put his clothes on without Thierry even turning over.

He paused before he left, looking down at the bed. Thierry was still sleeping, and he looked like an angel. The sheet had pooled around his waist, exposing his upper body, and Bishop couldn't help but smile at the sight of the hickey at the base of his neck. Even if Bishop didn't see him anymore, he would have a reminder of him, at least for a few days. Bishop wished he could say the same, but Thierry hadn't marked him. That was fine. He didn't need a mark to remember Thierry and what they'd done last night. He would always treasure the memories, especially when he felt alone.

He sucked in a breath, looked at Thierry one last time, then turned around and left the bedroom.

The house was silent as he moved through it. It was clean, just like Thierry. Everything was in its place, and there were no trinkets around, no mess. It was what Bishop had expected, and he couldn't help but smile. Thierry might not like that idea, but he was kind of predictable, and Bishop didn't mind. He loved predictable. He didn't want surprises in his life, not when the worst surprise he'd gotten was that his parents had died.

He paused at the front door, looked back one last time, then took a deep breath, and opened the door.

This was the last time that he would step out of this door, and that was okay. He would have to live with it, and he'd learn to. He'd learned to live with a lot worse over the years. He didn't look back, not even once. This was it for him and Thierry, and he needed to start getting used to that idea. The best way to make that happen was to forget Thierry existed, so he would try his best to do just that.

He knew it was impossible, though. Thierry was under his skin like a tattoo, and while his presence would eventually fade, he would always be there.

Thierry had suspected he would wake up alone, but that didn't mean it didn't hurt. It did, much more than he'd expected, much more than it should.

He rolled to his back and stared at the ceiling. When he and Bishop had kissed on the couch last night, he'd hoped there would be more for them. Even though Bishop had been clear that he wanted to focus on his sister, Thierry truly believed it was possible to love two people and take care of them. Bishop already did that, after all. He didn't merely love Ivy, but Carly, too, even though he didn't seem to realize that.

Thierry wanted Bishop to take care of him, too, but that might be too much to ask for.

He couldn't allow himself to stay in bed and mope. He shouldn't have opened his heart, even though it had only been for one night—one night of pleasure and feeling treasured. It had been a while since he'd felt that way, and he'd found himself hoping against all odds.

He'd been wrong.

Bishop might want him, maybe for more than sex, but he wasn't Bishop's priority, and from the way things had gone, he doubted he ever would be. He didn't know what would happen with Christmas dinner, but until Bishop mentioned otherwise, Thierry would assume that Bishop and his family would come.

He reached for his phone on the nightstand and quickly texted Bishop his mom's address. Then there was nothing else he could do. It was out of his hands, and Bishop would have to be the one to make the next move. Thierry couldn't say he was looking forward to it, mostly because he didn't want to wait. He hated not knowing what was going to happen next. He hated feeling helpless even more. He was in this situation, though. He and Bishop had spent a wonderful night together, but for Bishop, that was all there was to it. No matter how hopeful Thierry had been and how he'd opened himself up to Bishop, how he'd showed him a side of himself people didn't usually see, there was nothing else Thierry could do. He could only hope that Bishop would see how wrong he was not to allow anyone else in his life, and if he didn't, well, Thierry would have to get used to that.

He got up, even though he didn't want to. He showered, hating that he was removing Bishop's scent from his body but knowing it was a necessity. It was what it was, and it would be no use moping around and hoping Bishop would call. He wouldn't, not unless something changed. Thierry didn't think anything would, though. Nothing had changed in the past six years, not for Bishop.

Maybe Thierry just didn't understand what it was like to care so much about a sibling. He was an only child, and he'd never minded it. His parents had loved him, but they'd never spoiled him, and he'd been a happy child, even if a bit lonely at times. Not too much, though. He and his mother had a great relationship, and they'd been best friends when he grew up, even though his mother had also acted as a mother. They still had a good time together, and it was one of the reasons Thierry had been looking forward to spending Christmas with his parents. It was one of the reasons he'd lied to his mom. He wanted to make her happy, and apparently, that would only happen if he was happy.

He had been, for one evening. He'd allowed himself to hope, and he shouldn't have. It was over now, and since it was, he should focus on what was next.

Christmas dinner. Thierry could tell his mother that Bishop and his family had decided to stay home after all because Carly was sick. Then later, once the holidays were over, he'd explain that he and Bishop had broken up.

And Thierry would be alone in this house, having to watch Bishop come and go from next door. Because no matter what happened between them, Bishop's sister still lived in the house right next to Thierry's, and there was no way he could avoid her and Carly forever. There would be times when he and Bishop would see each other, and things would be awkward. That was okay, though. Things had been awkward between them in the beginning, too, but they'd gotten over it.

They would this time, too.

Chapter Six

Thierry hadn't seen Bishop since they'd spent the night together, and he wasn't sure he would see him again. So far, Bishop hadn't let him know if he was coming over for Christmas, so Thierry still had hope. It wasn't high, though. It was obvious that whatever was going on in Bishop's head, Thierry hadn't been able to break through.

What was worse was that Thierry missed Bishop. He shouldn't, not when they barely knew each other. He supposed that what he missed the most was what they could have had. In the beginning, it had been a lie, but during the evening they'd spent together, both with Thierry's mother and alone, Thierry had seen what the future could be like with Bishop in his life.

He wasn't one for relationships. Most people told him he was too complicated and high maintenance. They didn't want to have to deal with that, and he'd made his peace with it a long time ago. He'd thought Bishop got him, though. For one, he hadn't had a problem pointing out that Thierry was a chicken shifter, no matter what name he gave himself. He'd pushed until Thierry had to admit it, even though Thierry had pushed back. He didn't like it because people had terrible opinions about chickens, and most of the time, they were right.

But Bishop was gone, and Thierry had to go on with his life. Bishop had only been a blip in it, so it shouldn't be hard.

It shouldn't be, but Thierry couldn't deny how hard it was.

He headed to the garage to pick up his car. Luckily for him,

Pierce had only needed a few days to fix it, which meant that he would have it before Christmas. He sorely needed it. So far, he'd managed to get around by asking his mom to drive him, including to the grocery store. That meant he'd had to face a barrage of questions about Bishop—where he was, what he was doing, how long they'd been together, and many more. He hadn't known how to answer most of them. He wanted to tell his mom he'd lied, that Bishop wasn't really his boyfriend, but they *had* shared something. It might not have been a relationship, but they'd been close—for only one night.

Thierry also didn't want his mother to be disappointed by the fact that Bishop and his family wouldn't be coming for Christmas. Even though Bishop hadn't told Thierry they wouldn't, he'd lost hope he would spend Christmas with the man he'd started to fall in love with.

And that needed to stop, right now.

Thierry couldn't afford to fall in love with Bishop, or with the idea of what he'd made of Bishop. Bishop didn't want anything to do with him, and he had to wrap his mind around that, accept it, and go on with his life.

But he was nervous. Bishop might be there when he picked up his car, even though at this point, Thierry hoped he wouldn't. What were they supposed to say to each other? Should he ask Bishop if he and his family were coming over for Christmas? Should he act as if nothing had happened between them? He didn't know, which was one of the reasons he didn't do relationships. They were messy, especially when they ended.

But again, what he and Bishop had shared wasn't a relationship, was it?

Thierry stepped into the garage and looked around. He truly hoped he would manage to get in and out before Bishop noticed him but, but of course, Bishop was the one who moved away from the car he was working on and stepped toward Thierry. "Good morning, what can I do—" Bishop snapped his mouth shut when he saw Thierry.

Thierry looked away, trying to plaster a smile on his face and miserably failing. "I'm here to pick up my car," he said.

Bishop rubbed the back of his neck, then grimaced, probably because his hand was dirty. "Of course. Wait a moment."

He disappeared into the back office, only to come back alone a few seconds later. He didn't look happy, but he moved closer to Thierry. "Pierce will be right there with you. He's on the phone right now. He told me to keep you company."

Thierry snorted. "Keep me company? You mean like the other night, or like the morning after?"

Bishop's expression closed off. "What do you want from me?"

Thierry didn't know how to answer that question. "I don't know. What I didn't want was to be used as if I didn't matter."

Bishop grimaced. "That's not what I meant to do, and you know it. I told you there could be nothing between us. I told you that Ivy and Carly have to come first, and I haven't changed my mind. They need to be my primary focus. I can't have a relationship because it wouldn't be fair, either to you or to them. You have a family. We don't, and that means we have to stick together."

Thierry shook his head. He'd already told Bishop what he thought about that. He truly believed that people could love more than one person in their life and be fair to them without being unfair to others. It was obvious he wouldn't get through, though. Besides, how could Thierry be with a man who had already hurt him even though they weren't together?

He swallowed and forced himself to look at Bishop, even though there was nothing he wanted less. "You know what? Just forget about Christmas dinner. I'll tell my mom that we broke up. It's not like this would have worked anyway. We're too different. You're a fox, and I'm a French hen. You decided that you want to be an island against the world, and I can't do anything about it. I can't be anything for you, and that's fine. After all, it was just sex, wasn't it?"

Bishop winced, and Thierry knew it hadn't only been sex, not even for Bishop. There was nothing he could do with that information, though. Bishop had made his choice, and he wasn't going to change his mind.

Thierry stepped back. "I'll just wait outside. Tell Pierce I'm there when he's ready to see me."

"Thierry," Bishop began.

But Thierry didn't turn around to face him. He couldn't, not again. They might not have been together, but this felt like a break-up, and Thierry had never dealt well with those.

He just wanted to be loved. Was that too much to ask? Apparently, it was when it came to him. People either thought he was an asshole and didn't want anything to do with him, or if they did, they only wanted something quick and physical. People didn't love him for who he was, and he'd thought he'd come to terms with that. He had until he'd met Bishop, until Bishop had pushed his way into his life, until he'd made him see that maybe, just maybe, he could be loved.

But he couldn't. He should have known better, and now he was going to have to spend Christmas with his disappointed mom, and even worse, a broken heart.

CHAPTER SEVEN

Bishop turned around to make sure Carly was okay. She was still playing with her dolls, so he looked out the window again.

He was moping. He couldn't deny that, and he'd tried his best to stop, but he didn't think he could.

He missed Thierry. It didn't make sense, but he did, and he'd accepted that a while ago, almost since the moment he'd left Thierry's bedroom never to come back. And now, here he was, alone, on Christmas day.

He couldn't believe he'd messed this up, and in more ways than one. He'd promised Thierry he would help him with his mother, and now he wasn't keeping that promise. He'd thought he could give Ivy and Carly a real Christmas, a Christmas with family, and he wouldn't be doing that, either.

Was there *anything* he could do without messing it up?

He would try to make this the best Christmas Ivy and Carly could have, even though it wouldn't be easy. He was only one man, and they both deserved more. They deserved to have parents, people who cared about them, a family. Instead, they only had him.

Something fell on the floor, making him jump. He rolled his eyes. He had to stop moping. Yes, he and Thierry had shared an incredible night, but he'd always known it wouldn't go any further. He'd known that before he and Thierry had shared their first kiss, and he'd accepted it. Or at least, he'd thought he'd accepted it. Instead, he was still here, acting like he was never going to fall in love again.

He wasn't planning on doing that until Carly was at least eighteen. Besides, he wasn't in love with Thierry. He couldn't be, not when they didn't even know each other. The night they'd spent together didn't mean anything. It had only been sex, and Bishop knew it.

Except, he wasn't so sure about that anymore.

If he wasn't falling in love with Thierry, why couldn't he stop thinking about him? Why couldn't he put him to the back of his mind as if he didn't matter and never think about him again? Bishop couldn't fool himself. He knew it had nothing to do with Christmas and not being able to give his family what they deserved. On the other hand, it had a lot to do with how gentle Thierry was, how prickly, how sweet. He was a contradiction, and Bishop loved that. It made him want to push, to discover more about Thierry, to find what made him smile, what made him laugh, what made him cry.

But he'd fucked up that opportunity, and he knew it. Nothing he could do or say would change that. He might not know Thierry well, but that, he was sure of.

The front door opened, and Thierry smiled. His sister was home, which meant they could start celebrating. Carly had complained she was hungry a few times, and she'd soon cross the line into hangry if they didn't feed her.

"Where are my favorite people in the world?" Ivy called out.

"The living room," Bishop yelled.

She appeared at the living room door only a few moments later. She was smiling, even though she looked tired, and after a quick glance at Carly, her gaze zeroed in on Bishop. She grimaced.

Bishop wondered what was going on. "What?" he asked, getting up from the window seat. "Has something happened?"

Ivy shook her head. "*You* happened."

"What are you talking about?"

She looked at Carly, but Carly had barely waved at her when she'd come in. She was too busy playing. Ivy dumped her handbag onto the couch, then moved closer to Bishop. "What's going on?" she asked.

He wanted to lie. It would be the easiest thing to do, and it was tempting. He also knew that Ivy would kick his ass if he did that, though. That didn't stop him from trying. He didn't want to ruin Christmas. "Nothing's going on." He sat back down, hoping she'd let it go.

"That's bullshit, and you know it. Come on. Tell me."

Bishop sighed. "I don't want to burden you with my problems."

Ivy sat on the window seat next to him, crossing her arms over her chest. "Does it have to do with the neighbor?"

Bishop pressed his lips together. He wanted to ask how she knew, but that would make his interest in Thierry obvious.

Ivy chuckled and shook her head. "I knew it. I knew something was happening when I saw you leaving his house one morning. What's going on? Is he your boyfriend?"

"Of course not."

"What do you mean, of course not? I saw you leaving his house. It was obvious you spent the night together. Was it just sex? Or is there more to it?" She peered at Bishop as she waited for him to answer.

Bishop sighed. "It's more than sex."

"I can see that. You don't look happy, though. That means something's going on."

"Nothing is going on. We shared an evening, and that's it."

"Is that really it? Because you just said it was more than sex."

"What else could there be?"

"I don't know. I'm trying to get answers out of you, but you're not talking. That means something is going on, and I don't like it. I don't like how down you've been lately. You look like a kicked puppy. I want the truth, and I want it now, Bishop."

Bishop glared at her, but he'd always known that she would demand answers and that he would have to give them to her. She was his only friend, the most important person in his life. If he couldn't be honest with her, who could he be honest with? "It was more than sex, but there can't be anything between us."

"Why not? You don't like him? Apart from the obvious, of course."

"I like him just fine. I think I more than like him, actually."

Ivy's eyes widened, and she reached for Bishop's hand. "You're serious? You're finally falling in love?" Her smile fell. "But it's not going well. I can help you apologize and get him back, if you tell me more."

Bishop chuckled. "Why do you think I was the one who fucked up?"

"Because you're an idiot most of the time."

"I'm not an idiot. I told him there could be nothing between us, no matter the feelings. I have to focus on you and Carly. We're alone in the world, and you didn't deserve that. I already failed you six years ago. I'm not going to fail you again. I can't allow anything to distract me, especially not Thierry."

Ivy stared at Bishop for a moment. He wondered what she was thinking, but he didn't have to wonder for long.

She reached out and slapped him on the back of the head, hard enough to sting. He yelped and rubbed the spot she'd hit, glaring at her. "What was that for?" he asked.

"It's because you're an idiot, like I just said. Is this really the reason you can't have a relationship with Thierry? Because you think Carly and I need your protection, and you think you failed me?"

"It is."

"Then, again, you're an idiot, and possibly a bigger one than I thought you were. I don't need your protection, Bishop."

Bishop opened his mouth to point out that the last time he hadn't been up to do the job, she'd gotten pregnant and been abandoned by Carly's father. Ivy glared at him, prompting him to snap his mouth shut.

She nodded, satisfied. "And before you continue saying that you failed me six years ago, you didn't. I was an adult. I knew what I was doing, and I should have been more careful. But I loved her father, and I thought he was the one for me. I thought he would be happy that we were having a baby, even though we were so young. He wasn't, and that's on me, not on you. You can't choose the people I have relationships with, and I wouldn't want you to even if you could. You have to stop being a martyr about this. I can stand on my own two feet. I *have* been standing on my own lately, and you know why? It's because I realized that I've been leaning on you too much since Carly was born. I use you as a partner, and I shouldn't, because you're my brother, nothing more."

"I want to do this for you," Bishop said. He didn't want his sister to think that he regretted it.

"I know you want to, and I allowed you to because it was easier for me. But by doing that, I clipped your wings. I made you think that I needed you in my life and that you couldn't live your own because of that. I don't want that to happen. I want you in my life and Carly's, but I don't need you, and you should get your own life, possibly with Thierry, since you're falling in love with him. It's not fair for me to ask you to stick around, and I won't. I don't want to, Bishop. Actually, I think that after the holidays, I'll find a babysitter."

Bishop's stomach dropped. "You're taking Carly away for me?"

"I'm not taking anything away from you. I'm giving you

your life back."

Once again, Thierry would show up at his mom's house alone for Christmas. He hadn't told her yet, not wanting to disappoint her, but now, he realized he should have. At least if he'd told her on the phone, he wouldn't have had to see her expression. As it was, he would have to tell her face to face that he and Bishop had broken up, and she would be devastated.

He could imagine her in the house right now, flitting this way and that, making sure everything was perfect for Thierry, but more importantly, for his boyfriend and his boyfriend's family. And now, Thierry was about to tell her that Bishop wasn't coming, that there wouldn't be a little girl running around the house today. He knew his mother wanted grandkids, but he was an only child, and that was going to be impossible to achieve until he found someone to share his life with. He knew some people were great single parents, but he couldn't do that. He didn't have it in him, and his mom knew it. That was one of the reasons she'd never pushed for him to have children, but also one of the reasons she wanted him to find someone. The other reason was that she wanted him to be happy, but he was starting to wonder if maybe he should find happiness on his own. It was what a lot of people did, and it wasn't a bad thing.

Or rather, it wouldn't be a bad thing if he weren't so lonely.

He'd never realized it, or maybe he'd ignored it. That had been easier than to admit it to himself. But now he'd spent an entire evening and night with Bishop. He'd had dinner with him, had heard him talk to his mom, had heard them laugh together. He knew what Bishop felt like in his bed. He knew what it was like to roll over in the middle of the night and find someone there with you, warm and solid. Bishop hadn't been there when Thierry had woken up, but he had been for most of the night, and that had been enough for Thierry to want to continue sharing his bed. He'd always liked his space and disliked being restrained when he slept, but he found that when it came to Bishop, he didn't mind — much. He'd still slept on his side of the bed, which meant he'd made it easy for Bishop to sneak out, and he berated himself for that. Couldn't he have cuddled Bishop for at least one night?

He parked in front of his parents' home and stared at the house. So he was alone. That wasn't a problem. He'd been alone last year, too, and he and his parents had had a perfectly fine Christmas. There had been laughter, food, and happiness. This year wouldn't be any different. Once his mom's disappointment to find out that Bishop wasn't coming faded, she'd be happy. She'd always loved the holidays, Christmas in particular. Thierry couldn't give her a son-in-law or a grandchild, but he could give her love, and it was what he was going to do.

Still, he took his time getting out of the car. He gathered the gifts he'd put in the backseat, then, once he couldn't waste any more time, he took a deep breath and headed to the door. He knocked, not wanting to barge in, just in case his parents were making out under the tree or something like that. It had happened way too often for him to be comfortable walking into the house, even though he'd grown up here.

The door flew open, and his mom stood there, beaming. Her smile dimmed just a bit when she saw him on his own, but then, it perked back up. "They're coming with their own car? I should have known."

"Maman—"

"Bishop and his family. They're coming, right? I know he said he would have to check with his sister if it was okay with her, but I haven't heard anything from you, so I thought it was implied they were coming."

Thierry hated doing this, but there was no way out of it. He opened his mouth to explain, but before he could, her gaze moved to something behind him, and she pushed him to the side to welcome whoever was coming up the driveway.

Thierry turned around, and his jaw almost hit the ground when he saw Bishop parking his car. He hadn't even heard it, and he didn't know what was happening. Why was Bishop here? Was he only here for Thierry's mom and to make sure his family had a family Christmas, or for something else? Thierry was confused. He wanted to know what was happening, and he wanted to know it *now*.

He watched as Bishop opened his car door after saying something to the woman sitting in the passenger seat. They looked so much like each other that they had to be siblings, and Ivy was just as gorgeous as Bishop, albeit in a different way. She was softer, more feminine, but she looked just as strong and stubborn.

She was probably the reason they were here, now that Thierry thought about it.

Thierry's mom reached them, and she wrapped her arms around Bishop, startling him, if his expression was anything to go by. Still, he hugged her back, and he looked happy to do so. Then he turned around and gestured at his sister to come closer. He introduced Ivy to Thierry's mom, and Thierry could do nothing but stand there, staring. He had so many questions that he wouldn't know where to start asking them, but the most important one was what Bishop wanted from him. He had to know before he got his hopes up and before he allowed his mind and his heart to run away with this.

Ivy got Carly out of the car, and Thierry was pleased to see her again. She looked happy with her eyes wide as she took in the house. Thierry's mom had always been an over the top decorator, and this year wasn't any different. If anything, she'd gone overboard since she knew she would have guests and one of them was a little girl.

They reached Thierry, and Thierry couldn't stop staring at Bishop. Their gazes caught and held, and Thierry's mom chuckled. "Why don't we leave those two out here for a bit? I'm sure they'll want to say hello privately," she told Ivy.

Ivy smiled at Thierry. They hadn't even talked yet, but he could see he would like her. "We'll have time to talk and celebrate later. Bishop, why don't you stay here with him for a bit? Carly and I will head inside."

Bishop hesitated. "Are you sure?"

"I'm sure. And remember what we talked about."

Thierry pressed his lips together so he wouldn't ask what that was, but he was dying to know. He supposed he would find out soon enough, since Bishop obeyed his sister's order and stayed behind.

The front door closed behind the three ladies, leaving Thierry and Bishop to face each other in silence.

Bishop couldn't tell which way this would go. He wanted to think that Thierry would listen to him quietly, then be happy about the decision Bishop had made, but it would be in his right to tell Bishop to fuck off and leave. Bishop wouldn't be surprised if he did just that.

Still, he had to try. He had to make Thierry see that he'd thought about it and that he'd realized he was wrong. Ivy had helped a lot, and even though it would be hard, Bishop had agreed to take a step back. He would always be there for Ivy and Carly. He would always be Ivy's brother and Carly's uncle. But he wouldn't be in their life constantly anymore, not the way he'd been until now. He wouldn't babysit Carly every evening. He wouldn't be there every time Ivy had a problem, big or small. He hadn't realized it, but since they'd moved and Ivy had decided to rent a house for her and her daughter while he'd found an apartment, Ivy had started taking care of the house by herself. She was the one who took care of the rent and the utilities, and she dealt with the owner if something broke. Bishop had his own apartment, but he'd been spending so much time at Ivy's house that he hadn't decorated it.

Now was the time to do that.

And who knew, if things went right, maybe sooner or later, he would be moving right next door.

Before that happened, though, he had to apologize, and he had to make it good.

Thierry was still holding several gifts, but he put them down on the porch and crossed his arms over his chest. "I didn't think you would come," he said.

"I didn't think I would come, either, until a few hours ago."

"And you couldn't have called? Or at least texted if you didn't want to hear my voice? My mom still thought you were coming. If I'd known for sure that you weren't, I could have warned her."

"But you didn't, and she didn't even realize that something was wrong. Aren't you happy that she's happy?"

"You're an asshole," Thierry snapped. "Of course I'm happy for her. She's always wanted grandchildren, and she already loves Carly. That doesn't tell me what the fuck you're doing here, and I want to know right now."

Bishop knew it was stupid, but he was still tempted to tease Thierry. "What will you do if I don't explain myself? Punish me? Kick me out?"

"I'll tell my mom, Ivy, and Carly, that you had something to do. I can drive them home. It's not a problem, since I live right there."

Bishop was more amused than scared. "You sound like you thought about this quite a lot."

"That's because I did. You're an asshole, Bishop. Now tell me what you're doing here."

Bishop sucked in a breath. He was incredibly nervous, but Thierry was right. He deserved an explanation. "I talked to Ivy. She kicked my ass."

Thierry burst into laughter. "She does look like the kind of woman who would do that. And you deserved it. I'm glad she did."

"I'm glad, too. And I *did* deserve it. She made me see that I didn't fail her when she got pregnant. She was an adult and able to make her own decisions. And I won't be failing her by living my life. Actually, she told me that we needed to put some distance between us. She still loves me, and that won't ever change, but she needs to live her life, and I need to live mine. She's only twenty-five, and she has a little girl and a job. I guess that eventually she wants to meet someone and get married."

"You should have realized that a while ago."

Bishop shrugged and looked away. "I should have. But I was still grieving. I still am, in some ways. I guess I wanted things to go back to the way things were when our parents were alive, and being so close to Ivy and Carly helped with that. But they're gone, and they're never coming back. I can't have the past back the way I want it, but I can have a better future."

Thierry's expression softened, and Bishop hoped it meant that he was ready to give him a chance.

He pushed on. "So Ivy made me realize that there was space in my life for more than just her and Carly. There's space for you, if you still want me." There. Bishop said the words, and now, the ball was on Thierry's court. He was the one who would have to make the next decision—to take the next step.

It was terrifying.

"What do you mean by that?" Thierry asked because of course he was going to ask more questions instead of putting

Bishop out of his misery.

"I think that we can have something incredible together. Our only night together was, and it was just one night."

"Yet you snuck out of my bed without even waking me or leaving me a note."

"I shouldn't have. I panicked. I thought I was betraying the promise I made to Ivy to always be there for her."

"You don't think that anymore? I find it hard to believe."

"It's going to take me a while not to think that way. I can't promise I'll be perfect. But I'm going to try, and Ivy is, too. We've come to rely on each other too much since our parents died, and that means that neither of us has a real life. We both want that to change. She wants to stand on her own two feet, and she has been for a while. She just never pushed me out because she thought it would hurt me. We're all each other has."

"But that's not true," Thierry said softly. To Bishop's relief, he came closer and took one of Bishop's hands. "You don't only have each other anymore. Don't you see? My mom has already adopted your sister and your niece. You're part of the family, even if we're not together."

"It sounds impossible," Bishop confessed.

"I guess it would be for some people. But my mom's always been that way. She takes in strays, and I don't just mean animals. Besides, our immediate family is tiny. There's only three of us, and she's always wanted more. She wanted more children but couldn't have them, and now she wants grandchildren. I couldn't give them to her, not when I was alone."

"But you're not alone anymore?" Bishop's heart raced so much that he felt like he should press a hand over it so it wouldn't jump out of his chest and throw itself in Thierry's face. That would probably be the worst way to ask Thierry to go out with him.

"I don't know. I'm not sure what you're saying. I'm trying

not to hope too much, just in case I misunderstand you."

So Bishop needed to be more obvious. He pulled on the hand Thierry was still holding, and once he was close enough, he wrapped his arms around Thierry. He held him close, looking down at him. "Don't you see? I don't know why or how it happened, but I'm already halfway in love with you. I want more. I want to wake up every day with you by my side and not sneak out of the room and your life. I want us to have many date nights and many Christmases with your mom. I want everything with you." It might be too much, too soon, but Bishop might as well put everything out there. If it meant that he would have Thierry in his life, he was even ready to fall to his knee and propose.

Even though the idea of marriage was as terrifying as it was intriguing.

He didn't have to do that, though. Thierry smiled, and he leaned even closer. "That's what I want, too."

Those were the last words they said for a while. Bishop kissed Thierry, knowing that he would be able to kiss him again and again, without having to feel guilty.

He realized that things wouldn't be this perfect forever. But for now, he would take it.

EPILOGUE

Christmas had been perfect this year. It was always nice, but Thierry couldn't believe what a difference three people would make. He was happy he and Bishop were together, of course, but it was more than that. He could see it in his mom and even his dad. They were thriving with a child around them, and Thierry hoped this could become a yearly routine. He wanted them to be a family. He could tell his mom needed this, and now more than ever, he wanted to give it to her. He wanted to give her grandchildren to love and spoil.

It would take time, though, and in the meantime, she could spoil Carly. It looked like by finding each other, they'd all managed to fill voids they'd had inside—Ivy and Bishop needed parents, while Thierry's parents needed more children and grandchildren. Thierry wasn't jealous. He'd always known his parents had wanted more kids, and he'd always felt a bit guilty that his mom hadn't managed to, even though it hadn't been his fault. Now, he'd given her more people to care for, and he was happy. Even if things between him and Bishop didn't work, he could tell that they were still going to be a family. An awkward one, maybe, but family nonetheless.

The plus side of this was that he wasn't lying anymore. He'd told his mom that he and Bishop were together, and they were. He didn't plan on ever telling her that it had been a lie in the beginning. He didn't want to disappoint her, and he didn't want to have to explain why he'd lied. She would feel guilty, and that was the last thing he wanted. He understood why she'd pushed so hard, even though it had been irritating.

Bishop wrapped an arm around Thierry's shoulders and pulled him closer. There was plenty of space for them on the couch, but Thierry had been almost on top of Bishop since they'd settled there after dinner, and he wasn't about to move.

Bishop kissed Thierry's temple, then froze as if he wasn't sure he should have done it. Thierry loved it, though, and he couldn't wait to have more. He wanted to cuddle and watch TV together, to live through dusky evenings and happy summers. He wanted to experience everything with Bishop, and he thought he had a good chance of that happening.

"Thank you," Bishop murmured.

Thierry frowned and turned to look at him. "What for?"

"For accepting my family and me here. For not making things awkward. For welcoming me back into your life. I thought I would have to grovel a lot more than I did."

Thierry grinned at him. "Maybe you will. I haven't decided yet. It's going to be fun, though."

"For you, maybe."

"For you, too. Don't worry too much. Even if I do make you grovel, I'll make sure it's pleasurable." Thierry hoped his expression gave away what he was thinking about, and he thought he'd succeeded when Bishop's eyes widened and he smiled back.

There was a squeak, and they both turned around to see that Carly had shifted. She'd been playing with one of the toys Thierry's mom had bought for her, and of course, it was in the form of a fox. Now she was a fox, too, and she wiggled her ass before pouncing on the stuffed animal.

All the adults in the room laughed. The moment made Thierry think about the time in which Carly had pounced on him, and even though he'd been angry, he couldn't find it in himself to be any longer. It hadn't been the perfect way to meet Bishop, but it had brought them together. Besides, Carly was going to have to learn how to live around French hen shifters. She was part of Thierry's family now, and they would all help her master her shift and hide away from humans.

Thierry moved, and suddenly, Carly turned her attention to him. His eyes widened when she pounced on his shoes, closing her teeth around the tip and gnawing on it. It kind of hurt, so he snatched his foot back, but she tried to catch it again. He looked at Bishop, entirely lost, and Bishop laughed before reaching for Carly. He grabbed her under her front legs and hauled her up, and she looked as resentful as a fox pup could.

"We don't bite feet," Bishop scolded. He snapped his mouth shut and looked at Ivy, but she limited herself to smiling.

Thierry knew things would be awkward between Bishop and his sister for a bit. They had to find a new way to be with each other, but they would manage. Thierry knew that he, too, would have to learn to be around a family. He could already tell he would have to babysit Carly time and time again, but he found that he didn't mind. He didn't know how to deal with children, but that was mostly because he'd never had a child in his life consistently. Now, he did. He had a child, a boyfriend, and his family. He would learn.

He couldn't wait.

Bishop put Carly down and wrapped himself around Thierry again. "Sorry about that."

"Don't be. She's happy. She's having fun. We all are."

"Still, she shouldn't be biting."

"She didn't hurt me. I promise. Stop worrying about it. I'm more than happy to give her my shoe to gnaw on if that's what she wants. It's Christmas, after all. We should all get what we want."

"And what it is you want, then?"

Thierry reached up and kissed Bishop. "You, and I already

got you." It was a perfect Christmas, much more than Thierry had expected, and for once, he didn't mind that he'd been wrong.

ABOUT THE AUTHOR

Catherine is the creator of several series, most of them paranormal, including the Whitedell Pride Series and the Gillham Pack Series. While she graduated in translation, she decided to go the writer's way because it was more fun to create her own stories and characters.

She's been living in Italy for more than twenty years, but she's a daughter of the North—Belgium to be precise—and she misses it so much that she's already planning to move back.

She loves pizza—probably too much—her son, her pets, and of course, books. She sneaks some reading time into her schedule every time she has five minutes free from writing, demands from her various pets and son, and lastly, housework.

Connect with her:

lievens.catherine@gmail.com
BookBub: https://www.bookbub.com/authors/catherine-lievens
Website: https://authorcatherinelievens.com/
Facebook: https://www.facebook.com/catherine.lievens.9
Facebook Group: https://www.facebook.com/groups/411788002341528/
Twitter: https://twitter.com/authorCLievens
Newsletter: http://eepurl.com/c-uvKn